First thing this morning, the posters had gone up all over town. 'MORE DARING THAN EVER!' they'd said in blue and gold letters. 'WATCH MONSIEUR MERCURY DEFY GRAVITY ON HIS TRAPEZE!' To me, M. Mercury was good old Jasper, who I lived with in a tiny trailer, who drank lapsang tea out of dainty cups and let me have first dibs on every piecrust. Which was more than could be said for my mam. When I was just a baby she left me at the circus, the way most people forget an umbrella.

Praise for *The Girl Who Walked on Air*:

'An adventure of old-fashioned charm.' *Sunday Times* Children's Book of the Week

'Engaging and entertaining.' *Independent on Sunday*

'Terrific for encouraging middle-grade girls to be strong, brave, and happy in their talents.' *Evening Herald*

'A wonderfully rich, historical adventure starring a plucky heroine.' *WRD*

BY THE SAME AUTHOR

Frost Hollow Hall

ABOUT THE AUTHOR

Emma Carroll is a secondary school English teacher. She has also worked as a news reporter, an avocado picker and the person who punches holes into filofax paper. She recently graduated with distinction from Bath Spa University's MA in Writing For Young People.

The Girl Who Walked on Air is Emma's second novel. She lives in the Somerset hills with her husband and two terriers.

THE GIRL WHO WALKED ON AIR

Emma Carroll

FABER & FABER

First published in 2014
by Faber & Faber Limited
Bloomsbury House,
74–77 Great Russell Street,
London WC1B 3DA

Typeset by Faber & Faber Ltd

Printed in the UK by CPI Group (UK) Ltd, Croydon CR0 4YY

A CIP record for this book
is available from the British Library

ISBN 978-0-571-29716-0

4 6 8 10 9 7 5 3

For my parents,
who gave me books, not ponies

'Life is always a tightrope or a feather bed. Give me the tightrope.'

EDITH WHARTON

✳ FIRST ACT ✳

Chipchase's Amazing Aerialists

CHAPTER 1

The bigger the danger, the bigger the crowd. One look at tonight's punters said it all. With just minutes till show time, the big top was almost full and I was quite ready to burn with excitement. Every last ticket was sold. And still the queue snaked out of the field and down the lane until all you could see were people's hats bobbing above the hedgerows.

First thing this morning, the posters had gone up all over town. 'MORE DARING THAN EVER!' they'd said in blue and gold letters. 'WATCH MONSIEUR MERCURY DEFY GRAVITY ON HIS TRAP-EZE!' To me, M. Mercury was good old Jasper, who I lived with in a tiny trailer, and who drank lapsang tea out of dainty cups and let me have first dibs on every piecrust. Which was more than could be said for my mam. When I was just a baby she left me at the circus, the way most people forget an umbrella.

Inside the ticket booth where I worked there wasn't

space to swing a cat. I felt it specially tonight, jiggling from foot to foot, impatient to get finished so I'd be free to watch the show. My dog Pip sensed it too; sat beside me, he watched my every move. At last, the final punters filed past to claim their tickets. They were a noisy bunch, laughing and nattering, their breath like smoke in the evening air. They'd be quiet soon enough. Once they were inside the big top, they'd squeeze onto a bench and look upwards. And what they'd see would leave them speechless.

A little shiver went down my neck. *Imagine if I was about to perform. All those eyes gazing up at me. Just imagine it!*

I came back to earth with a bump. The circus owner, Mr Leo Chipchase, was in the doorway. He'd put on his best tartan waistcoat and was smiling, which made a change.

'Think of all those backsides on seats, Louie,' he said as he squeezed in beside me to count the takings. 'The bigger the danger . . .'

'. . . the bigger the crowd,' I finished for him.

He did have a point. There were grander circuses than ours, with more animals, more curiosities, more sparkle. Backsides on seats mattered. So, what better way to draw the crowds than a thrilling new routine.

And tonight that's exactly what they'd get. Jasper would perform not a double but a TRIPLE somersault from his trapeze. No other circus boasted such a stunt. It was genius.

But it was dangerous too. Now I'd reminded myself of this fact, it grew like a little worm inside my head. Tonight's show had that *whiff of death* all right. How anyone could hang mid-air for so long I didn't know. Jasper made it look easy. And I thought of Charles Blondin – the GREAT Blondin – who'd crossed Niagara Falls on a *tightrope*. One hundred *thousand* people had turned up to watch him. They placed bets that he'd fall and die. He didn't, of course, but I still felt sick thinking about it.

At last, the queue ended.

'Can I go now?' I asked, for my fidgeting had got worse.

If I was quick, I'd get to wish Jasper luck. And be sure of a good viewing spot at the back of the big top.

Mr Chipchase waved me away. 'Go.'

I darted across the showground straight for the big top. Smells of horse sweat and gingerbread filled the air. There was music too, the organ and drums all fast and furious, signalling the show was about to start. It was the bit of circus life I loved best, that moment before the action, when the very air tingled. And tonight I felt it keenly. How I dreamed of being a showstopper like Jasper. Breathed it. Lived it. But on this subject Mr Chipchase was clear. 'Not a chance, Louie,' he always said. 'You're too young.'

Never mind that Mighty Ned the ringmaster was my age. Or Kitty Quickblade, who threw knives, was only a tiny bit older. But when I'd pointed this out Mr Chipchase went red enough to burst.

So these days I watched from the sidelines. And I kept my dreams to myself.

*

I realised now that Pip wasn't with me. Cupping my hands to my mouth, I yelled his name. He came hurtling towards me like he'd been fired from a cannon, a terrier-sized blur of white with one brown ear.

'You little monkey!' I said as he squirmed at my feet. 'Now stay close.' He had no sense of occasion, this dog of mine.

To reach the big top we had to pass Miss Lilly's fortune-telling tent. She stood in her doorway. ' 'Tis a strange night,' she said as I went by.

'Evening to you too, Miss Lilly,' I said. 'Must dash.

I can't miss Jasper's performance.'

'Very wise,' she said. 'A great change is on the way. The cards are predicting it.'

She often came out with this queer stuff. It was fine with her punters as they'd paid for a tarot reading, but I didn't want to hear it. Not tonight.

I rushed on. Behind the big top was a roped-off patch of grass. It was abustle with horses and jugglers and performers limbering up. In the centre of the space a bonfire blazed, making the dusk seem darker than before. It made me blink. And run smack bang into Kitty Quickblade.

'Watch it, weasel!' she cried.

I hated her calling me that. What she meant was, 'You're not like us, you're not proper circus,' because I had pale skin and green eyes and hair the colour of cinnamon, which no one else here did.

She tossed back her own dark curls, hands on hips. 'What do you say?' she said.

Her tunic glittered in the firelight. It was all my handiwork, for when I wasn't selling tickets I mended costumes. I'd sewn every last silver sequin of this one till my fingertips were raw. It looked magnificent. But I'd never got as much as a smile for my trouble. Or a decent wage.

I gritted my teeth. 'Sorry, Kitty. I didn't mean to.'

Really I wanted to wallop her one. But Kitty was Mr Chipchase's daughter, which meant I had to mind my manners.

Since I'd grovelled enough, she let me past. I ducked inside the tent, Pip at my heels. The space backstage was the size of a small courtyard and brightly lit. Dusty velvet drapes separated us from the main ring. Yet the smell of sawdust was just as sharp, the ooohs and aaahs of the crowd as clear. We might've been out in the ring ourselves. It made the hairs lift on the back of my neck.

In the middle of everyone was Ned the ringmaster. Done up in his top hat and scarlet tailcoat he looked awful smart. Especially since out of costume he was all elbows and giant feet.

'Almost time, showpeople!' he cried, then seeing me he dropped his voice, swaying like he might faint. 'Wish me luck, Louie.'

'You great idiot.' I shoved him hard, for we were like that, Ned and me, always mucking around. Lately I suspected he'd gone soft on me. I hoped he'd snap out of it soon. 'My luck's for Jasper, not you.'

Except I couldn't see past Rosa the bareback rider, or Marco and Paolo the clowns. The place was filling up fast. There was no sign of Jasper. I started to panic. Time was running out. And I still hadn't wished him good luck.

In the ring the crowd had gone quiet. The drums rolled. Ned stepped through the curtains. 'Ladies and gentlemen . . . girls and boys . . .' he boomed. 'Tonight we have a most marvellous show . . . a show where . . .'

A hand touched my shoulder. I spun round to see Jasper, looking every inch the showstopper. His dark hair was slicked back and his costume sparkled green and red. There was nothing of the *whiff of death* about him; he was all puffed up strong like a lion.

'Everything all right, Louie?' he said, bending down to stroke Pip, who wagged his tail.

'Just excited for you.' And I was too. My stomach fluttered madly.

Jasper straightened up. 'Here's to good luck, then,' he said, reaching for my hand. He kissed my palm three times, same as we did before every show.

'I'll keep them safe till afterwards,' I said, closing my hand to a fist. Once the performance was over, I'd give him the three kisses back. It was our ritual; it brought us luck. Always.

The curtains parted.

'Tonight . . . defying gravity . . . I give you . . .

Monsieur Mercury!' Mighty Ned cried.

The drums beat faster.

Jasper went up on tiptoe then stepped forward. The curtains closed behind him. I waited for the lights to dip, then peered through a chink in the fabric. Marco let me stand in front of him. He said he'd see fine over the top of my head. Pip sat on my feet, his little body trembling. I hardly dared breathe.

High up in the roof, Jasper flexed his arms. As he waved to the crowd, his tunic flickered in the lights. It made me think of dragonflies. Then he put rosin on his hands and gripped the trapeze. As the crowd went completely hushed, my own mouth turned powder-dry.

Jasper started easy. Slow and sure, he swung from one side of the tent to the other like a clock part. He tucked his knees over the bar, let his arms trail then folded himself over. The drumbeats slowed. It was almost restful. I breathed again.

He went faster.

The music kept pace. He swung this way. That way. Now he was a blur of colour. His legs were stretched out straight. Then he flipped upwards. He let go of the swing and somersaulted twice before grabbing the trapeze again. He did it once more. Then spun backwards. The crowd gasped. Though I'd seen his routine in practice, I couldn't take my eyes off him. Nothing else mattered. A spell had been cast over us all.

Then Mighty Ned spoke. 'And now ladies and gentlemen, for the triple somersault, the most daring trick of all . . .'

The drum roll seemed to go on and on. Jasper stretched his whole body, swung low and wide, gaining momentum. The magic of it held me fast. He reached high up into the roof. At the very top of the arc he let go. He spun once, twice, three times and seemed to hang in the air. Then he reached for the trapeze.

And missed it.

He fell to the ground like a shot bird.

CHAPTER 2

In an eye blink, it was over. Jasper lay still on the floor. Deep within the crowd the screaming started. The screams became shouts became groans of horror. Mr Chipchase rushed into the ring, with Kitty and Paolo in his wake.

'Don't look,' said Marco, trying to shield me.

But I had to see. The crowd was on its feet, surging for the exit. I tried to squirm free from Marco's grasp. Pip started yapping at my ankles.

'No Louie, stay back!' Marco said.

I clawed at his arm until he loosened his grip. In a flash, I ducked through the curtains.

A huddle of figures stood in the middle of the ring. Just as I reached them, I stopped. Mr Chipchase looked over his shoulder. He saw me and stepped back to let me through. Yet my feet didn't want to move.

I took a deep breath. Shut my eyes for a second and told myself to be brave. My legs shook as I shuffled forwards. The group of people closed around me. It struck me as strange: here I was in the centre of the ring. Everyone was watching me. In a funny way, I was the star of the show. How I'd hoped for such a moment. How I'd dreamed of it.

Yet never in the world like this.

It was safer to gaze at Mr Chipchase's waistcoat, with its thick golden watch chain and buttons straining. He had an arm around Kitty's shoulders. For once they weren't even bickering.

'I don't know what went wrong,' Mr Chipchase said.

I supposed he was speaking to me.

Eventually, I looked down. There was no blood. Jasper lay on his side like he was sleeping. His eyes were shut, his hand tucked sweetly under his cheek. The only strange thing was the way his feet twisted outwards.

I sank down beside him. A lock of stray hair had fallen across his forehead. I smoothed it tidy; he'd have wanted to look neat, even now. Then I took hold of his hand and, turning it over, gave back his kisses.

One. Two. Three.

I waited for the pain to hit. No one spoke a word. We must have stayed like that quite some time, for when I looked up, all I saw was a wall of legs. They seemed to press in on me. I found it hard to breathe.

The legs shifted. Hands pulled me to my feet. An arm went around me. It was Rosa the bareback rider, and suddenly I was glad to have someone holding me.

'Should we get a doctor?' I said.

Everyone looked to Mr Chipchase. He'd let go of Kitty and was dabbing his face with a handkerchief.

'Sadly, that won't be necessary,' he said.

The group fell silent. Outside, a horse whinnied. A steady tap tap on the canvas told me it had started to rain.

Suddenly Rosa stiffened. 'I don't believe it!' She was pointing at Jasper. 'He moved!' she cried. 'I swear to you, he's just moved!'

I seized Jasper's hand and leaned in close to his face.

'Jasper? Can you hear me?'

Nothing.

'It's me, Louie.'

Not a flicker.

I didn't have the strength to get up. I held Jasper's hand, imagining all the love draining out of me and flowing into him. It felt stronger than saying it out loud. I might have been there a minute, an hour, even a whole day. At some point, I felt a tickling against my palm. I thought it was my own fingers moving.

Then I realised it wasn't. Jasper opened his eyes.

*

Paolo was sent to get a doctor from town. The other men lifted Jasper onto a hurdle and carried him back to our wagon. He was properly awake now, and the tiniest movement made him cry out in pain.

Once inside, we got Jasper into his bunk. It wasn't easy since the bed was narrow, and to reach it the men had to turn sideways. There was much gasping and grunting, and even when Jasper was finally safe in his bed the weight of the blankets were too much for him to bear.

The doctor came from town quick enough. His first order was for the crowd outside our wagon to leave. 'Except those responsible for the care of this fellow,' he said.

That left just me and Mr Chipchase, who looked like he'd rather go too. I began to feel nervous myself. The doctor introduced himself as Dr Graves. It wasn't a very cheering name for a person in his line of work, but everything else about him was purposeful and neat, right down to his well-trimmed whiskers. He ordered me to bring him water to wash his hands in, so I stoked the stove and put a pan on to heat. Then after removing his jacket and hat and cleaning his hands, he began his examination.

'Easy, my good man,' said Dr Graves.

There were many sharp gasps; I winced at each one. Thankfully, it didn't take long for the doctor to reach his conclusions.

'He has a bad fracture to his pelvis. There's a break to his right thighbone too. How exactly did this happen?'

I shivered as Mr Chipchase explained. 'He fell a good sixty feet.'

'And how did he land?' asked Dr Graves.

'On his right-hand side.'

'How long was he unconscious?'

'About fifteen minutes.'

'Hmm . . . did he know you when he came round?'

'He knew Louie here. Didn't let go of her hand.'

They both looked my way. Then the doctor rummaged in his bag, pulling out a little brown glass bottle. He gave it to me.

'Mix this with a cup of warm water. Let's say thirty

drops. It'll take the edge off the pain.' Then, to Mr Chipchase, 'I'll need your help to set the bone in his leg.'

There was a silence.

'Come now,' said Dr Graves. 'It's a two-man procedure. The sooner we get it done the better.'

Mixed with the drops, the water turned a reddish brown and smelled bitter. The doctor took it from me and propped up Jasper's head so he could drink it. Some of it spilled from his mouth but mostly he swallowed it down, eyes tight shut. Soon he was drowsy. The doctor removed the blankets and Jasper's costume without too much flinching.

'Now, sir,' said Dr Graves, turning to Mr Chipchase. 'If you could just step over here . . .'

But Mr Chipchase had gone as pale as raw pastry. He backed towards the door. 'I'll find someone else for you,' he said, and was gone.

The doctor cursed under his breath. He looked at me. 'Will you do it? Before the laudanum wears off?'

I nodded. He bid me stand at Jasper's shoulder. I glimpsed a twisted limb, bulging above the knee. The skin was shiny-tight. It hardly looked like a human leg at all.

'Put both hands around his thigh, and grip it hard,'

said Dr Graves. 'And when I count to three, pull backwards with all your strength.'

There wasn't time to be squeamish. I gripped. Dr Graves took hold of the lower leg in the same way. Jasper groaned, twisting his face into the pillow.

Dr Graves bit his lip. Little drops of sweat had formed on his brow. 'One . . . two . . . three . . .'

I heaved with all my might. The doctor pulled in the opposite direction, turning the leg as he did so. Jasper screamed. There was a grinding noise. Beneath my hands I felt the bone shift. Something creaked.

'Enough!' cried Dr Graves.

I glanced down. Jasper had passed out cold. Yet his leg was now a thing to behold, stretched out straight as a train track.

'Good work,' said the doctor, admiringly.

My face, I supposed, looked astonished, for he then spoke sharply, 'Quickly now, pass me those bandages.'

I did as I was told, though I couldn't help grinning. It was rare that I got the chance to show I might be more than a ticket-selling, costume-mending nobody.

Once Jasper was all bandaged up and sleeping soundly, the doctor made ready to leave.

'You are his daughter, I assume?' he said.

It wasn't a mistake easily made, not with my red

hair, though I did have Jasper's surname of Reynolds. And if anyone asked, I'd say, 'I'm his niece from the country,' which was what I did now. So far it'd kept me safe from the orphanage.

The trailer door swung open. Mr Chipchase's great bulk filled the doorway.

'You're too late,' said the doctor. 'The bone has already been set.'

'Managed by yourself, eh?' said Mr Chipchase, who clearly hadn't found anyone to help and looked relieved to be let off the hook.

'I was most ably assisted by his niece here.'

I felt pleased as punch. Or at least I did until I saw the shock on Mr Chipchase's face.

'What, *Louie*?'

I scowled at him. The doctor hadn't thought me too young to help *him*. There were things I was good at, and not just mending broken legs. If only Mr Chipchase would give me the chance.

The doctor put on his hat. 'We managed well. Now, if you'll excuse me, I have other patients.'

'Wait!' Mr Chipchase seized the doctor's arm. 'Can we move him tomorrow?'

'That wouldn't be wise. He needs complete rest.'

'But we can't stay put! We're a travelling show!'

It was true. We never stayed longer than two nights anywhere.

'Then you'll need to make an exception,' said Dr Graves, removing Mr Chipchase's hand from his arm.

'And if we do stay, will he be back in the ring soon?'

The doctor looked horrified. 'I hardly think so!'

'But Jasper's my star performer. He has to get well. The show won't make money without him,' said Mr Chipchase.

'That man,' Dr Graves said, nodding at Jasper, 'is lucky to be alive. If he walks again – and I mean *if* – I predict he will have a profound limp.'

A limp wasn't much, not really.

Yet Mr Chipchase's face said otherwise. This wasn't good news, not to a circus. Jasper was our showstopper act. Mr Chipchase stroked his side whiskers: this wasn't a good sign either.

'What are you telling me, doctor?' he said.

The wagon seemed suddenly chill.

'I'd start looking for another star performer, Mr Chipchase,' he said. 'Jasper Reynolds's days as an acrobat are over.'

*

Once the doctor was gone, Mr Chipchase cleared his throat. He shifted uneasily from one foot to the other, making the plates rattle on the shelves.

'What is it, sir?' I said, for I reckoned this was about Jasper.

He stroked his whiskers. 'Louie, we took you in as a baby and now you're a . . . well . . . quite a bit older.'

'Yes,' I said, thinking he'd not win any prizes for observation.

'Jasper was a good earner for this circus. And, as you know, we're not a big venture. Not like . . .'

'Wellbeloved's,' I cut in.

'Exactly.'

Wellbeloved's was a big, flashy circus, and Mr Chipchase's pet hate. He mentioned them when times were tough, and always in the same bitter tone.

'So,' he continued, 'money will be tight. And if Jasper can't work for us, then . . .' He raised his palms.

'What?'

'You'll have to do more around here.'

'I'm game,' I said. 'You know I am.'

But Mr Chipchase frowned. 'Taking you in hasn't made life easy for us. Even to this day there are . . . *issues*.'

I didn't quite follow.

'Speak plainly please, sir.'

He rubbed a hand over his face. 'All these years, I've expected someone . . . to claim you,' he said slowly. 'But they haven't.'

I eyed him nervously: what *someone*? Though I knew from the tightness in my chest exactly who he meant. I hardly needed reminding of how *forgetful* my mam was when it came to me. Still, this new information hurt like a slap.

'My mam won't come back for me, sir,' I said, eyes stinging. 'Ain't any point thinking she will.'

Mr Chipchase looked taken aback. 'Louie, I don't . . .'

'She was glad to get shot of me, sir, truly she was.'

He went tight-lipped. I hoped that meant we were finished, for I'd nothing more to say on the matter.

'We'll care for Jasper as best we can,' he said. 'But the doctor's right . . . what this circus needs now is a new showstopper.'

'Yes sir.'

'And you, young lady will need to earn your keep. *More* than your keep from now on.'

'Yes sir,' I said again, trying not to smile. For surely he'd just solved his own problem.

CHAPTER 3

That night I couldn't sleep for trying. Then just before dawn my eyelids grew heavy. And – *bam* – Mr Chipchase's words exploded in my brain. Fancy him expecting my mam to come back! Didn't it prove what she thought of me, that she'd forgotten I existed? I lay stiff and cross under the blankets. Pip opened one sleepy eye at me then went back to snoring. By now I was fully awake.

Jasper slept on in the opposite bunk. Quiet as I could, I lifted a corner of my mattress and pulled out my scrapbook. It was stuffed with newspaper clippings, all of which were on the same topic. I'd learned my letters from the headlines, though I still got stuck on certain words. Spreading the book across my knees, it fell open on my favourite page. The headline alone got my heart pounding: 'BLONDIN ROPE DANCES ACROSS NIAGARA.'

Glued on the page was the grainy picture of a man

on a high wire. The Great Blondin himself. He stood with his left leg tucked behind him, balance pole across his knees. Every time it struck me – how tiny he looked! A rocky gorge reared up behind him. On the river below boats passed by like dots. Yet it was impossible to look anywhere but at him. He gave off magic, a kind of hope. It was as if he was walking on air.

This magic flickered inside me like flames. If Blondin believed the impossible, then so could I. And it wasn't *that* impossible, not really. With a shiver, I thought of Miss Lilly, who last night said she foresaw a great change. Normal times I'd have shrugged it off, but things *were* changing, so fast it made my head spin. Chipchase wanted a new showstopper: I had a talent to offer. Put like that it sounded simple. All I had to do now was make him listen.

*

Sunrise was the best time for practising. Once I'd watered the horses and tipped their oats onto the grass, I fetched my rope. For months now I'd hidden it in the belly box of our wagon. Heaped in with the horses' harnesses, Jasper hadn't noticed it was there.

This morning the horses looked dozy as they ate. Not me. I was wider than wide awake, the fluttering in my stomach quite strong. I'd dressed in one of Jasper's old tunics. It beat tucking up my skirts like I usually did. But then today wasn't usual. Not by far.

Next job was to wake up Ned. And that was never ever easy.

He lived with his mam, Rosa, the bareback rider. The remains of last night's cooking fire still smouldered outside their wagon. Me and Ned had our own special knock, of a kind adults seemed unable to hear. I did it now, a tap-tap-tap with just my fingernail on the side of the trailer, right near where he slept. I waited. And waited a bit more.

'Come on lazy bones,' I muttered under my breath.

An age seemed to pass. I knocked again. Even Pip started to look bored. Finally, the door opened. Ned appeared, still wrapped in a blanket.

'What's going on?' he said blearily. Then his face fell. 'It ain't Jasper is it? Nothing's wrong?'

'Jasper's passable,' I said. 'Now listen. I need your help.'

'What's that rope for? And what the heck are you wearing?'

I sighed impatiently. 'All you have to do is watch.'

*

Twenty minutes later I was ready. No one had ever watched me before, only Pip – and that didn't quite count. Jittery though I was, I trusted Ned to be straight with me. He saw all the acts go in and out of the ring, so he'd know a star turn if he saw one.

The rope was now tied between two stout trees, about ten feet off the ground. I'd climbed up there myself while Ned watched from the ground. He thought it was all one big prank. Right up until I kicked off my clogs, tied back my hair and asked him for a leg-up onto the rope.

'You ain't getting up on *that*?' he said in amazement.

'Of course I am, stupid. Now help me up.'

'You're stark raving.'

'I will be in a minute if you don't help me!'

'It isn't safe, Louie. You can't just get up on the rope and . . . well . . . *do it*. It's a proper skill. It takes years of practice!'

'Yes,' I said. 'I know.'

I could've told him about my scrapbook. About Blondin, my hero. And that while he, Ned Bailey, had been snoring away in his cosy bed, I'd been practising

26

every morning for as long as I could remember. But I wanted him to see it for himself.

'Help me up,' I said.

'No.'

I narrowed my eyes at him. 'If you don't help, I'll tell everyone you're sweet on Kitty Chipchase.'

He glared at me. Then he put his hands around my waist.

'Not like that,' I said, wriggling out of his grasp. 'Do it like I'm getting on a horse.'

So he cupped his hand for my foot and on the count of three he heaved me upwards. I moved onto the rope till I lay flat across it. Slowly, I eased myself into a crouching position. Now I was a lot taller than Ned. The thought made me giggle. Or maybe it was just my nerves.

'I've got a bird's-eye view of the top of your head,' I said.

'And I've got a gentleman's-eye view of your ankles, pretty miss,' said Ned, putting on his posh ringmaster's voice.

'Stop it,' I said, giggling again. 'Now step back and watch.'

'Shouldn't I stay here? Just in case you fall?'

'You're a pea-brain, Ned. 'Course I won't fall.'

My mind went quiet. I stood up slowly, counted to five and focused straight ahead. The entire world had shrunk right down to this one length of rope. Nothing else existed. Under my feet the rope swayed slightly. It was part of me now. It had grown out of my heels and toes. We were the same thing, this rope and me. It made me feel wonderfully light.

Arms out to the side, I took a step forward. Then another. Left foot, right foot, sliding forward along the rope. When I reached the other side I stopped. Turned right round to face the way I'd come. The only movement was in my ankles as they worked to keep me upright. I started walking again, this time making more of a show, flourishing my wrists, stopping to crouch down and stretch out each leg in turn. It felt good to be watched. It made me think harder about how I moved, what shapes and lines I made.

When I reached the middle the rope began to sway. Not badly, but enough to make me steady myself. I didn't have a balance pole; I made do with outstretched arms. Bending my knees a little helped too. Slowly, surely, I kept moving, the rope always a part of me. As it grew still again, I spun on one foot like a dancer. Below me, Ned breathed in sharp.

Eventually, at the other side, I leaned on the tree trunk and grinned down at him.

'What d'you reckon?'

His mouth hung open. 'Do it again,' he said. 'Blimey, Louie! Do it again!'

Pip barked excitedly and ran round in circles. The flames were there again inside me. Now I'd started, I wanted more. More people, more cheers, more gasps of delight.

Focus, Louie.

A deep breath, a thought of Blondin above that great ravine and my mind cleared. I stepped out onto the rope, spread my arms and walked as if I was strolling in the park. Then I turned right round and did it all again.

Finally Ned said, 'You better come down.'

Back on the ground, I felt suddenly shy in my too-big tunic and Jasper's old tights. Ned seemed unable to speak.

'Sorry I got you out of bed,' I said, once we'd untied the rope.

Ned stayed silent, his hand dragging slowly down his face. 'I've never seen the likes,' he said eventually. 'I bet even Wellbeloved's ain't got anyone like you.'

He sounded like Mr Chipchase. It made me grin.

'Wellbeloved's has got EVERYTHING. We ain't in the same league,' I said.

'If you say so.'

'But am I any good?' I said, impatient now.

He took my hand, squashing it between both of his. 'You're better than good. You're blooming brilliant!'

'Really?'

He nodded eagerly. 'Why didn't you tell me before?'

'I had to be sure I could do it,' I said. 'And Jasper would have kittens if he knew what I'd been up to.'

'He'd have stopped you most probably,' said Ned, for we both knew Jasper worried more than twenty mothers.

I laughed. 'He could've tried!'

'Where d'you get a talent like that from though, Louie?'

I stopped laughing. 'It's *my* talent,' I said, taking my hand away from his. 'It doesn't come from anywhere else.'

'Maybe it's in your blood.'

I'd much rather Ned kept telling me how good I was. I didn't much fancy talking families.

He leaned close to me, putting on a silly,

storytelling voice. 'Maybe your mother was a famous performer in a far-off land . . .'

'Stop it.'

He pulled a face. 'I was only playing.'

'My mother abandoned me here, and that's all I know – all I *want* to know,' I reminded him. 'Jasper's my family. I don't need anyone else.'

'I didn't mean to . . .'

'And as far as I'm concerned, my mother ain't anyone fancy, so there's no point pretending she is. I don't even know her name.'

We fell quiet.

'Ta for watching me,' I said eventually. 'You're the only person who has.'

He grinned. 'Just wait, Louie. You'll be filling that big top in no time.'

It was impossible to stay cross at Ned for long. 'D'you think so?'

'Too right I do!'

And he shouted for all the world to hear, 'Mr Chipchase! Call off the search! Your new showstopper is right here!'

CHAPTER 4

Whistling for Pip, I went to Mr Chipchase right away. There was the smallest chance he hadn't heard Ned's great gob, and I'd far rather tell him myself. Yet the second I saw him my heart sank. He was standing at the top of his wagon steps. Last time he'd said no to me he'd been wearing the same red-spotted waistcoat. This time he was busy saying no to someone else.

A man and a woman stood below Mr Chipchase on the grass. In their stiff, dark clothes they looked like townsfolk. And they didn't exactly seem happy. Bursting though I was, I knew better than to interrupt. As I stepped back their voices became raised.

'*A spectacle?* It was horrific!' the woman cried. 'That poor man perished in front of five hundred people!'

'He didn't die, you foolish woman!' Mr Chipchase retorted. 'Jasper Reynolds survived!'

The man wrote something down in a notebook.

'That'll make the evening papers if we're quick,' he said.

So the man was a reporter. Mr Chipchase caught sight of me just then and his face went from red to pale.

'Not now, Louie,' he said through gritted teeth.

The reporter and the woman turned round. Pip trotted over, bold as could be. He sniffed the woman's skirts. She tried to push him away, all the while staring at me like I was some sort of freak.

'A child performer,' she said. 'I should've known.'

As I went to claim Pip, she started with the questions. Proper daft ones they were.

'Have you been whipped, poor soul? When did you last eat? Are you forced to work all hours?'

Tucking Pip under my arm, I scowled at her. She was a do-gooder, I could tell by her dull grey coat and the sharp look in her eye. Types like her made things tricky for girls like me. They kicked up a stink about young performers. Any second now she'd insist I needed rescuing and put in a proper school.

Well, she could try.

She held out a gloved hand to me. 'I'm Mrs Dorothea Grimstone, secretary of the Society for Moral Obedience.'

I didn't take her hand. Unsure what to say, I glanced at Mr Chipchase. His face had gone red again.

'Never mind Louie. She sells tickets,' he said, which made me scowl even more.

The reporter eyed me up and down. 'Really?'

'I hardly think so in *that* costume,' said Mrs Grimstone. 'And she has striking hair. How unusual.'

Mr Chipchase marched down the steps. He stood between me and Mrs Grimstone, shielding me from her gaze. 'We have no child performers here. If you're set on investigating then try Wellbeloved's Circus,' he said. 'Now good day to you both.'

As soon as they'd left he turned to me. 'What are you playing at, you foolish girl?'

' I . . . I . . . was . . . um . . .' I shifted Pip onto my hip. My moment of asking to be a showstopper had very definitely passed.

'Do you realise the harm you could've caused?'

'But I . . .'

'The last thing we need is *you* all over the papers.'

I glared at him. '*Me?* They wanted to know about Jasper, not me!'

Sighing heavily, Mr Chipchase put a hand to his brow. 'Yes, I suppose so.'

He went quiet and I thought he'd finished.

Not so.

'Jasper's accident has got people talking,' he said. 'With reporters and busybodies sniffing around, we need to watch our backs. There are people out there who hate the circus. An accident like this just gives them more to crow about.'

'I was only . . .'

'If that Mrs Grimstone thought for one second you really were performing here she'd try to close us down.'

'She wouldn't!'

'Damn it, girl, of course she would! Times are changing. People want danger, but not if it puts a child at risk.'

'What about Wellbeloved's? You said they use children.'

He flinched. 'The less you know about that circus, the better.'

Yet he'd brought up Wellbeloved's, not me.

'So the sight of you appearing dressed up like some . . .' he rubbed his forehead, '. . . some child trapeze artist, well, it hardly helped.'

'It ain't dangerous if you train yourself properly.'

Mr Chipchase looked at me in disbelief. 'Tell me you haven't been *training*.'

'Might've been.'

'Oh great heavens alive,' he groaned. 'Training at what?'

'Um . . .' My mouth went dry. 'The tightrope.'

His face dropped a mile.

'I'm very good at it,' I said, all in a rush. 'Ned's seen me and he says I'm . . .'

'No,' Mr Chipchase said firmly. 'Not the tightrope. Absolutely not.'

'Just watch me and then decide.'

'No. That's my final word.'

As he turned to walk away I grabbed his arm. 'Please, Mr Chipchase, sir, it could be just what we need to get business going again.'

He shook his head. It made me think of Jasper's leg: he'd not believed I'd helped mend that either.

'I can do things,' I said. 'I'm not a dimwit.'

'Really?' He shrugged me off. 'I want you OUT of the papers, not IN them.'

I blinked back tears. It wasn't fair. I'd never be a showstopper at this rate. 'Just give me a chance,' I begged.

'Did you not hear what that woman said? And the reporter too? The pen is mightier than the sword, Louie. If we put you up on a high wire, they'd roast us alive!'

'But you said you'd find me another role.' I started to get frantic. 'And this is what I'm good at.'

'I said NO!'

'But I . . .'

'Enough! Now get out of my sight!'

*

Back at our wagon Kitty Chipchase was waiting at the door. She was the last person I wanted to see.

'What is it?' I said, trying to hide the fact I'd been crying.

She thrust her silver tunic at me. 'It's split at the shoulder. Sew it better this time, weasel.'

Putting Pip down on the grass, I took it from her. My tears sprung up afresh. Stupid me for thinking I might walk the tightrope like Blondin. This was all I was fit for, mending Kitty Chipchase's poxy costumes.

'Is that it, then?' I said, for she hadn't moved off.

She put her hands on her hips. 'Not quite. A word of warning to you.'

I tensed up. This wouldn't be pleasant. It never was with Kitty. She seemed to begrudge me the very air, and I'd no idea why.

'I saw you,' Kitty said. 'Just so you know.'

'Saw what?'

'I woke up early this morning. And guess what sight greeted me?'

I stared at my feet.

'I saw you. On a tightrope. With Ned Bailey watching.'

My cheeks went *whoosh* with heat.

'You were good. A bit too good. But don't get above yourself, weasel. Papa'll never make you a showstopper. You've had enough favours out of him already.'

I didn't say a word. I went inside the wagon. Shutting the door behind me, I picked up my needle and thread and got to work like a good girl. But my mind was set. One day I'd walk that tightrope and the world would watch in wonder. I wouldn't be put off, not by do-gooders, not by Kitty Chipchase.

Not by anyone.

CHAPTER 5

Just as Mr Chipchase feared, the evening papers weren't kind. 'TRAPEZE ARTIST IN TERRIFYING PLUNGE,' they said, and worse, 'CHILD USED AS REPLACEMENT ACT,' which wasn't even true. It was a bitter blow, and hardly helped my case. Yet Mr Chipchase rose above it. He put on his tartan waistcoat and declared tonight's performance would be a paper house show, which meant free tickets for all. Despite the headlines, few punters could resist. The big top was full in no time.

And to my very great surprise, I was asked to perform.

My excitement lasted all of ten seconds.

'It's a simple routine,' Mr Chipchase said. 'How hard can it be?'

Aghast, I'd tried to tell him. 'Sir, please, Pip can't do tricks. He ain't that sort of dog.'

Which was putting it politely. Wild foxes were

more obedient than my Pip. But Mr Chipchase's mind was set. There'd be no high-wire walking, not even a trapeze, just safe, sweet things to win the punters over. And Pip and me doing tricks was part of the plan.

Even Jasper saw the funny side, though it hurt his ribs to laugh. 'You two, a buffer act? Crikey! Times are hard!'

He was closer to the truth than he knew.

My costume didn't help. I'd found myself a blue satin jacket and top hat, packed away in a trunk. It wasn't perfect but with my hair brushed and gleaming, I looked quite the part. So did Pip in his matching bow tie. Yet Mr Chipchase was horrified.

'Great god! You'll be recognised!' he cried.

'I thought that was the idea.'

Weren't we showing a child performer all safe and happy? Weren't we trying to prove the do-gooders wrong?

'Find yourself a clown suit,' Mr Chipchase ordered. 'And for goodness' sake cover up your hair.'

So waiting backstage, I felt nervous AND ridiculous. The only clown suit I'd been able to find was the vilest shade of horse-dropping green, with arms and legs so long I had to roll them up. Mr Chipchase also insisted I plait my hair and hide it under a hat. The whole get-up made me hot and prickly. Not so Pip, who seemed quite at ease in his bow tie.

In the final seconds, I went over our routine: *dog walk, dead bodies, murder hunt, justice.* Mr Chipchase was right: how hard could it be? If this went well tonight, it might lead to bigger things. Anything was better than selling tickets and sewing for Kitty Chipchase. Even Blondin must have started somewhere.

Through a chink in the curtain, a blur of horse went past. Rosa was on her last lap of the ring. The crowd roared in delight, whooping and whistling and slapping their thighs. I tried not to think of last night, and the different sounds the crowd made then. The curtain flicked open. Rosa appeared, pink-cheeked as she clapped her horse Moonbeam on the neck.

'Didn't he do well?' she grinned, sliding to the ground.

I must have looked dazed because she nudged me.

'On you go then.'

I glanced down at Pip. He fixed his eyes on me. One nod and he trotted into the ring like he was off on a morning stroll. I tucked our props under my arm and went after him.

The lights in the ring were fierce. I'd seen them hundreds of times, but being underneath them made me blink. The smell hit me too: sawdust, damp grass, animal sweat. And the stench of five hundred bodies all cramped together on benches around the edge of the ring.

Only the very front row was lit. We called this the pit; it was where the posh sorts sat, and tonight all the seats were taken. Ladies dressed in their finest silks sat with men in top hats. There were children too, eating toffee and swinging their legs.

Mighty Ned cleared his throat. 'Ladies and Gentlemen . . .'

I took my spot, ready as I'd ever be. Pip sat at my side. Putting down my props, I gave my head a quick scratch. This hat was awful itchy. The crowd was still buzzing from Rosa and Moonbeam's equestrian skills. They hadn't quite noticed us yet, so I did what I'd seen the other performers do; I waited for the punters to settle. That moment of shifting and rustling felt like forever.

I kept still, my heart going boom boom inside me. But Pip was getting restless. He yawned, showing the speckled inside of his mouth. Then he put a paw over his eyes and lay down. People cottoned on. They started to laugh.

Mighty Ned joined me in the middle of the ring, facing the audience with his arms spread wide, turning slowly so everyone saw his bright scarlet coat. The hubbub died away.

'And ... now ...' said Mighty Ned, pausing between words for that extra bit of drama, 'ladies . . . and gentlemen . . . be amazed . . . be *very* amazed. For here we have a dog who can . . . really and truly . . . SOLVE CRIME!'

'Ha ha! Believe it when I see it!' some charlie called out.

'Now then . . . a little respect, please . . . because ladies and gentlemen . . . I give you . . . THE GREAT DOG DETECTIVE!'

A roll of drums, a smattering of applause, and the tent went silent. The limelights were on me.

This was it!

Smiling to the crowd, I flourished my arms. The knot in my belly loosened a little. First, we did a lap of the ring, while Mighty Ned took charge of the storytelling.

'One fine day, a girl and her dog went for a jolly little walk.'

The crowd went 'aaah' at Pip, all jaunty at my side.

'Everything was splendid until . . .' A drum roll

43

sounded, '. . . they took a shortcut through the woods. Soon they were lost.'

The audience 'ooohed' and 'aaahed' some more.

'Watch yourself, girlie!' someone cried.

It was working: they seemed to like us. I allowed myself a little smile. We walked down the middle of the ring, Pip weaving in and out of my legs. A flick of my hand and Pip stopped. I gave him the eye and he spun round on the spot, once, twice and then stood still. The crowd clapped.

Good boy. First trick done.

I felt myself glow with pride.

The lights darkened. Inching nearer the props, I reached out with my foot for the straw-stuffed sack that served as a body. I hesitated, thinking of Jasper. Last night he'd been lying here for real. It wouldn't do to think of that now. With a quick kick, I positioned the sack where I wanted it, in a heap at the edge of the ring.

'*It was night-time*,' Mighty Ned went on, '*so the girl and her dog decided to get some sleep.*'

I lay down on my side. The audience chuckled. Opening one eye, I saw Pip standing over me, looking worried.

'Lie down!' I hissed.

He wagged his tail.

'Down!'

Someone in the front row rustled a toffee paper. Pip's head swung round. I gritted my teeth.

'Pip!'

He looked at me again, reading my face, and laid himself down like he was meant to.

'But something woke the little dog. He spied a person hiding in the trees. The person ran away, but what he'd left behind . . . was . . . a . . . BODY!'

A click of my fingers and Pip sprang to his feet. He set off across the ring, barking and yapping till he found the 'body'. He was meant to stand by it, paw raised, looking clever. Instead, he shook it like it was a giant rat. The crowd laughed. Grabbing hold of the other end, I hissed at him to drop it. But to him it was all a game and he dug his teeth in deeper. A ripping noise soon followed. I fell backwards with half the sack in my hands. The audience roared. I wanted to die on the spot.

Quickly things went from bad to worse. Pip got bored and wandered off. The audience grew tired of us too. People turned in their seats to speak to friends in the crowd. Some started slow clapping and calling out names. I took my bows with a heavy heart.

*

Back at the wagon, Jasper was awake.

'Well?' he said, propping himself up on one elbow.

'Don't ask.' I tugged off the wretched clown suit, flinging it onto my bunk. 'It couldn't have gone worse.'

'It was your first show. Tomorrow should be better.'

I snorted. '*Tomorrow?* This was my big chance to impress Mr Chipchase and I've ruined it.'

'There'll be other chances, Louie.'

Jasper was trying to be kind, but it just made me crosser. 'Not likely! That's the end of it for me.'

I yanked on my nightgown and wrenched my hair from its stupid plaits. Then I sat by the stove, staring at the ashes. Slowly, I began to calm down. Maybe Jasper was right; tomorrow might be better. And if it wasn't, then I'd have to convince Mr Chipchase of my real talent, if only he'd let me use it.

Behind me, Jasper winced. I felt awful guilty then for tending my own silly thoughts.

'Don't fuss,' he said as I went to help him sit up.

'Huh! That's rich coming from you.'

Once I'd got his pillows comfortable, I made us a pot of tea, and cut the rabbit pie Rosa had brought by. We ate far too much of it, or at least Pip and me did.

And as I licked my fingers clean then settled down in my bunk, everything seemed a little bit better again.

Then, out of the blue, Jasper said, 'I'm sorry you're having to look after me, Louie. It's supposed to be the other way round.'

I rolled over to face him. He lay staring up at the roof.

'We look after each other,' I said. 'You're my family, Jasper, so that's how it works.'

Except it didn't, not with my real flesh and blood who'd abandoned me. I tried to push the thought from my mind.

'What's the matter, Louie?' said Jasper.

He looked directly at me now. I reached for his hand but couldn't quite meet his eye. 'I'm all right,' I said. 'Pip and me need more practice, that's all.'

'This isn't just about dog tricks, is it?'

My stomach turned queasy. Maybe it was the pie. Or maybe it was because I'd never told him about the tightrope. It was my secret. Though now Ned knew of it, and Mr Chipchase and his rotten daughter, it was hardly a secret at all. Yet if I told Jasper he'd only fret. Better to wait until he was well.

'You say I'm your family,' Jasper said, 'yet we never talk about your real family, do we?'

I stiffened. 'No.' Pulling my fingers free, I got out of bed.

'Perhaps it's time we did,' he said.

This was far worse than talking tightropes. I started slamming plates onto shelves for a distraction. Pip slithered under my bed. Behind me, I sensed Jasper waiting for an answer. 'Not tonight,' I said.

Or any other night.

I'd nothing to say about her, that woman who'd left her own child with strangers. She'd forgotten me. And I'd best forget her.

'Perhaps tomorrow, then,' said Jasper.

'I don't think so.'

'We could at least try . . .'

'Why?' I picked up the teapot and banged it down again. 'Mr Chipchase told me she was meant to come back for me. So where is she, eh?'

Jasper sighed. 'I don't know. But you mustn't give up hope. She might still return.'

'Don't make me laugh!'

By now I'd run out of things to slam, so I shook my blankets. Jasper reached out and took my arm, forcing me to stop and face him.

'That's enough, Louie.'

Letting go of me, he sank back on his pillows. I sat

down. For a while neither of us spoke. Eventually I said, 'Do you want some more tea?'

'No.'

'Your medicine?'

'Not yet.'

'What, then?'

'I want you to be happy. Good things will come along, you'll see.'

I took his hand again. 'But you're my good thing, Jasper.'

It was enough. Almost.

There was no point feeling sorry for myself. Things were changing around here; I mustn't forget it. Jasper would get well again. And Mr Chipchase might finally listen and make me a showstopper.

Yet what if Jasper was right and Mam did come back? I felt a sudden rush of panic. Some things were too much to hope for. Thinking this way was no use to anyone.

CHAPTER 6

Ten days later, Mr Chipchase sent Ned and me to the post office. He'd advertised for a showstopper in *The Era* magazine, and now he wanted the replies. Kitty hadn't taken kindly to this news; her face was even more sour than usual, which was no mean feat. For once I knew exactly how she felt.

Yet today I was fed up for a different reason: I was waiting for Ned. He'd been standing across the street, nattering to some gent in a carriage, for what felt like the last five *years*.

'Oh come on, Ned!' I yelled. 'Any time before Christmas would be grand!'

One question had gnawed away at me for days now. And I couldn't settle till I knew the answer. If some stranger was to get the very job I wanted, then I had to know *who*, even if it did hurt like hell.

Ned ignored me. He kept talking and shrugging his shoulders as though he had all the time in the world. It occurred to me then that I didn't have to wait. I could sign for the post myself! Far as I knew, there was no law against it. No one had died and made Ned king of letter collecting. I tied Pip's lead to a lamp post so he wouldn't wander off, then I went inside.

There was a single counter with bars across it and a blue sign saying 'Telegrams' on the wall. Straightening my shawl, I went up to the counter. Behind it was a bald-headed man in shirtsleeves. He wore an eyeglass, so I wasn't sure where he was looking.

'Excuse me, sir,' I said.

'You're from the circus,' said the postmaster.

So he *was* looking at me then, not the rack of writing paper to my left.

'Yes, and I've come for our post, if you please.'

He raised an eyebrow. 'You'll have to sign for it. Write your own name, can you?'

'I ain't no idiot, sir,' I said, trying my best to stay polite.

He grunted then slid a form and pen under the bars. I did a big squiggly signature and passed it back. The postmaster frowned at it, then turned to rummage among the shelves. I stood on tiptoe to watch.

How many replies did we have? Hundreds?

Thousands? For who wouldn't want to be the showstopper act at our circus?

I jiggled from one foot to the other. This man was even slower than Ned. He was intent on checking every single piece of mail.

'Hurry up,' I muttered under my breath.

The postmaster finally turned round. 'Not much, I'm afraid,' he said, passing me the letters.

I stared at them in disbelief. There were three measly replies. THREE. 'Well, ta anyway,' I said and stuffed them in my pocket.

Out in the street, Ned was still conversing with his gent. It didn't help my mood. Nor did the sight of Pip, who'd wrapped his lead twice around the lamp post and looked about to choke on it. Quickly, I untied him and set off down the road. I'd had enough of waiting for Ned.

No sooner had I started walking than the fancy gent's carriage rumbled past. It sent up a great cloud of dust. Ned then appeared at my side. 'Where you off to?' he said.

'Got fed up hanging about for you,' I spluttered, waving away the dust.

'Missed me, more like.'

'Hardly!'

Ned was a bit too smarmy these days. It was starting to get on my wick.

He stopped dead. 'Knickers! We forgot the post.'

'You might've. *I* didn't,' I said, waving the letters at him. He looked put out, which made me a tiny bit pleased.

We turned into the main street. A coal cart was parked up on the corner, and a boy jumped down from it with a bag slung over his back. He seemed in a hurry and soon overtook us on the road. He kept looking back over his shoulder too. Eventually, he disappeared out of sight.

'What did that gent in the carriage want?' I asked Ned.

'Just asking questions. He was looking for someone. All sounded a bit odd. Anyhow, what about those letters?'

I showed him the envelopes again but didn't let him take them, not yet.

'Blimey, there ain't many of them,' he said.

By now, we'd left the village and were heading towards the river where the circus was pitched. Up ahead of us was the same boy who'd jumped off the coal cart, though my mind was still on the letters.

I pulled Ned into a gateway. 'Let's have a quick look.'

'I dunno, Louie. They're Mr Chipchase's letters, not ours.'

'Thought you'd be up for it.'

'Just don't blame me if he notices.'

Once I'd got a fingernail under the flap, the envelopes opened easy enough. My hands shook as I unfolded the first letter. It was a three-page missive in a tiny, spidery hand. I'd go cross-eyed trying to read it, plus I didn't know half the words. Also enclosed was a proper studio portrait done on card, the *carte de visite*. Every star performer had one.

'Oh my word!' I gasped, showing Ned. 'Look at that!'

The photograph was of an enormous woman in her undergarments.

'Blimey! Is she real?'

The horror on his face made me giggle. 'Dunno. What d'you think?'

He peered at the photograph then shook his head. 'Nah! That's a walrus in a corset, that is.'

We both fell about laughing.

The next one wasn't much better. There was no letter, just the *carte de visite*. This time the photograph showed a man hanging on to a trapeze. He had a huge white beard and legs like string. He'd easily be ninety years old if he was a day. 'A trapeze artist? At his age?' I snorted.

'I reckon he's already dead,' Ned said.

The final letter was from a man and his dancing bear. At least, I supposed the man had written the letter, though it could've been the bear since the writing was worse than a child's.

'Mr Chipchase doesn't do exotics,' said Ned, meaning the bear. 'And can you imagine living with that brute?'

The bear didn't look savage. He looked plain miserable. In my eyes it was the man with his big whip that was the brute. And by now I'd seen enough. I folded all the letters again. Sealing them the best I could, I gave them to Ned. 'Mr Chipchase'll be disappointed,' I said.

'Don't look so glum. It might work out for you, this.'

'How, exactly?'

Ned raised one eyebrow, then the other. I didn't laugh. But I did cotton on. The applicants were useless. Anyone could see that. It might just strengthen my case. 'You're a cunning creature, Ned Bailey.'

'Let me put in a word for you,' said Ned.

But I still didn't think it would help. 'It's them do-gooders.' I sighed. 'What with them banging on about child performers and me looking a bit young. I'm scuppered before I even start.'

'Then I'll tell Mr Chipchase I've seen you perform.'

I shook my head. Things weren't that easy. The Great Dog Detective act had gone from bad to worse, so I was hardly flavour of the month. And since Jasper's fall, every single show had lost money.

'*Do* let me tell him,' Ned pleaded. 'I'll say how brilliant you are, that you'll be the best showstopper he's ever seen.'

'If anyone's doing it, I'd rather tell him myself,' I said.

Ned kept on. 'He does listen to me . . . well, sometimes. So just leave it to me, Louie. I'll sort it out for you. You'll be charming the crowds in no t— . . .'

'Stop!' I cried.

It was too much. This was *my* business. *My* dream. I didn't want it becoming something else. Ned looked at me like I'd slapped him. I suspected he fancied himself as my knight in shining amour. But I didn't need one of those.

'Buck up.' I gave him a playful nudge. 'Now, which of these three gets the job?'

Soon we were joking again about the walrus woman and the dead man swinging from the trapeze. As we turned into the showground, I stopped mid-laugh.

Standing by the ticket booth was the same boy who'd walked past us on the road.

'Who d'you reckon he is?' I asked Ned.

'Come for an early ticket, I expect.'

'I'd best find out.'

Ned went off to Mr Chipchase's wagon, whistling and slapping the letters against his thigh. I prayed he'd keep his good words to himself. Then I turned my attention to the boy. He crouched down to greet Pip first, and did so like a person who truly loved dogs. This softened me a little. It also gave me a chance to size him up. I reckoned he was older than me, though only just, and tidily dressed in a collarless shirt, dark jacket and trousers. He had summer-blond hair and freckles across his nose. His chin was a bit too sharp and his eyes a bit too green, but all together it was a very nice face.

'You wanting something?' I smiled in what I hoped was a friendly way.

The boy stood up and took off his cap. This made me smile more. People didn't often take their caps off for ticket sellers like me.

'The man in charge, if you please.'

He was a flattie, a not-from-the-circus person. Or at least he spoke like one, all posh and proper. He had manners too, and he looked at me when he talked.

'Mr Chipchase is the gaffer here,' I said.

'Very well. Then that's the fellow I wish to speak with.'

'Who shall I say's asking?'

'Gabriel Swift.'

I giggled. 'That's a fancy name, that is!'

He stared at me like I wasn't right in the head. I stopped giggling at once.

'Wait there,' I said.

Pip sat down next to Gabriel Swift's bag. 'Not you, you great ninny,' I said and dragged him away by his collar.

First stop was our wagon to get rid of my pesky dog. Next stop, Mr Chipchase.

I found him at his desk, looking sullen. Kitty was there too. They'd clearly just had a barney; half of it still hung in the air.

'What's *she* wanting?' Kitty said as I came in.

There were three scrunched-up envelopes on the floor. So Mr Chipchase hadn't thought much of the replies to his advert either. Maybe Ned was right, that this would work out. I felt suddenly braver. Once Mr Chipchase had seen to this boy, I'd ask him outright. I'd make him listen. I'd show him what I could do.

'What is it, Louie?' Mr Chipchase said irritably.

I'd almost forgotten why I was here. 'Oh . . . yes. Some flattie person wishing to see you, sir.'

'Well, I *don't* wish to see anyone,' he said, and went back to his paperwork.

'Says he's called Gabriel Swift.'

Mr Chipchase went still. Then he sat forward in his seat. Kitty's face fell.

'But what about me, Papa?' she wailed. 'Can't you consider *me*?'

He held up his hand to silence her, then turned to me. 'Gabriel Swift, you say? *The* Gabriel Swift? Didn't he have a brother?'

'Dunno, sir. How many Swifts are there?'

Mr Chipchase didn't answer. He was already halfway out the door.

CHAPTER 7

I admit I was rather curious, and set off after Mr Chipchase. He was crossing the showground at quite a pace.

'So who's this Gabriel person, sir?' I asked, once I'd caught up with him.

'He's from Wellbeloved's, but don't let that concern you,' he said gruffly. 'He's one of their finest performers. I can't imagine why he's here.'

But I could. Or was beginning to. I'd got a cold sinking feeling inside.

As he saw us approaching, Gabriel Swift greeted us with a smile. Mr Chipchase shook him by the hand.

'And what brings you here, young man?' He sounded almost wary.

Gabriel smiled some more. 'Mr Chipchase, sir, I'd be honoured if you'd consider me for your show.'

I groaned silently, my fears confirmed. So much for him being a flattie.

Mr Chipchase looked intrigued. 'Really?' he said, stroking his side whiskers. 'Hmmm, I see.'

He made a play of considering it, but I saw the glint in his eye. And with Kitty's wail still ringing in my ears, I knew there was little chance now of Mr Chipchase choosing me; I was just another person in the showstopper queue.

Yet why hadn't this Gabriel Swift person answered the advert by post, like he was supposed to? What made him so special?

It wasn't hard to answer. He had such a graceful, upright bearing; Jasper had it too. *Or had it once*. Now all he had was a broken leg and a very uncertain future. Meanwhile, Mr Chipchase's whole face had lit up; I knew he was thinking about money.

'Very good, young man!' he said, now rubbing his hands rather than his whiskers. 'And Mr Wellbeloved knows you've left?'

'Oh yes. That's been resolved.'

My heart sank another notch.

'May I ask how?'

Gabriel ran a hand through his hair. 'He's doing more shows in America these days.'

'America, eh?'

Mr Chipchase seemed impressed. And so was I.

America . . . America! Even the word made me shiver.

'Very good,' said Mr Chipchase, all smiles. Then his face fell.

'Is there a problem, sir?' Gabriel asked.

Mr Chipchase shook himself as if waking from a doze. 'What? Oh, no . . . Only,' he paused, 'Mr Wellbeloved doesn't know you've come to *us*, does he?'

'Why no, sir.'

'Good. It would be better if he didn't. In fact, we should give you a new stage name altogether.'

Now I knew about circus ways, that you didn't poach another show's star turns. And Mr Wellbeloved was a big name, capable of causing big trouble.

'A new name, a new start,' said Gabriel.

'Splendid!' Mr Chipchase clapped him on the shoulder.

That was it then. The deal was almost done.

What Chipchase's Circus needed was someone with star quality, and here was just the person, offering himself on a plate. And he'd come to us – *little old us* – from a circus as grand as Wellbeloved's. There was no point in me asking Mr Chipchase anything now. My chance of being a showstopper had gone.

'Show us what you've got then, Master Swift!' he said.

I'd still no idea what Gabriel Swift's talent was. Despite everything, I decided to stay and watch.

Inside the big top, bright sunshine turned the canvas into a glowing dome of blues and golds. It looked magical. A tingle spread upwards from the soles of my feet and I began to feel a tiny bit excited. Finding myself a quiet seat in the corner, I waited for the action to start.

Marco and Paolo were ordered to set up a rope. They hurried up and down ladders. Mr Chipchase shouted instructions till his face turned scarlet. There was no sign of Kitty; I supposed she was sulking somewhere else. Gabriel, however, watched everything. So did I. Very soon I realised what was happening.

It couldn't be. Could it?

There was no mistaking it.

What I was looking up at – *oh my heart* – was a tightrope. And Gabriel was about to walk along it.

Tears welled up in my eyes. Hot, angry tears they were too. For how dare this *boy* come from nowhere and steal my place? It was like pouring salt on a wound. Yet I couldn't move from my seat. I kept staring upwards, transfixed by the rope, all the while thinking, *he'd better be good*. Because if he wasn't it

63

would make it ten times worse.

Gabriel stood in the centre of the ring. From his bag, he took out what looked like lengths of a fishing rod. One by one, he connected them together until they made a curved pole that was easily fifteen feet long. Then he held the pole lightly in both hands and placed one foot in front of the other, walking like he was already on the tightrope.

I slumped down in my seat and folded my arms. *Huh! And he had fancy equipment too!*

Blondin used a pole in all his stunts. It helped with balance. But balance poles cost money. And ticket sellers like me didn't earn thruppence, so I had to make do with spreading my arms wide and hoping to heaven I didn't fall.

Gabriel warmed up for another few minutes. And then, when he finally looked ready, he knelt on the ground and kissed it. I sat forward. *A good luck ritual.* It made me think of Jasper. And though I wanted to, it was one thing I couldn't scorn Gabriel for. It showed he knew the risks.

Moments later, Gabriel was at the top of the ladder. He knew we were all watching him. It fed him somehow, made him grow bigger, stronger. I understood that feeling. I'd felt it myself when Ned had watched me. And as he stepped out onto the wooden platform, the excitement made me shiver. I couldn't help it.

Everything went quiet. Gabriel's power came from his feet, laid toe to heel on the rope. He barely lifted them at all. Instead, they seemed to slide like he was skating. His knees were slightly bent and he held his arms a little away from his body. He faced forwards, eyes not moving from a spot up ahead. The pole moved in slight dips and sways. Gold and blue sunlight flickered off him through the big top canvas. He looked as sure as a bird. He wasn't a job stealer anymore; he was a creature of magic.

When Gabriel reached the other side he stepped onto the platform and gave a bow. Then he walked backwards along the rope to the point where he'd started. I was transfixed. Any second now he'd spin round or do a stunt with props. Or even something madly daring. Something with the *whiff of death*.

He didn't get the chance.

Mr Chipchase boomed 'Bravo! Bravo!' and I realised I'd forgotten to breathe properly.

Gabriel sat on the tightrope, one leg tucked under him and the other dangling downwards. He might've been sat on a wall.

'What tricks can you do, young man?' Mr Chipchase said.

It wasn't enough just to rope walk anymore; not since Blondin with his cooking routines, his wild animals, his walking inside a sack. Once he'd even carried his manager across Niagara Falls. Though I didn't think Gabriel would manage to carry Mr Chipchase – the rope would snap first.

Gabriel's leg stopped swinging.

'Certainly I can do tricks,' he said, though he didn't exactly sound keen.

It was on the tip of my tongue to cry, 'Show us then!' But it seemed Mr Chipchase wanted to draw things to a close.

'Perfect. Let's get you signed up,' he said, dabbing his face with a handkerchief. 'What's good enough for Gideon Wellbeloved is good enough for us.'

In Gabriel's shoes I'd have punched the air and whooped, but he simply shut his eyes and breathed deep. He looked sort of . . . *relieved.*

'And you're sure Mr Wellbeloved doesn't know you've come to us?' Mr Chipchase said again.

Gabriel opened his eyes. 'Absolutely, sir.'

'Marvellous. When can you start?'

As Gabriel climbed down the ladder, the spell broke

completely. Proper pain spread through me. I watched as Mr Chipchase shook Gabriel's hand. I didn't notice Ned slip into the seat next to me.

'Great on that tightrope, wasn't he?' he said, sounding a bit off.

I glanced at him. He was chewing the inside of his cheek.

'Gabriel was terrific,' I said. 'You don't seem so sure.'

'You're better.'

I smiled weakly. It was a kind thing to say but it wouldn't help now. 'I missed my chance,' I said. 'And so has Kitty. She won't be happy either.'

Ned shrugged. He stuffed his hands in his pockets and turned away.

'What's up with you anyway?' I asked.

'Nothing.'

'Don't believe you.' For he honestly looked like someone had stolen his last penny.

Ned huffed about in his seat a bit more. He really wasn't himself. More to the point, I still had half an eye on Gabriel and Mr Chipchase. And Ned sitting here grumping was blocking my view.

CHAPTER 8

So Chipchase's Travelling Circus had a showstopper once more. It took some getting used to. Yet my dreams hadn't changed because of Gabriel Swift, or 'The Great Fun Ambler' as he was now known. If anything it made things clearer.

The next day wasn't a moving on day, so there was time to practise. Pip and me got up at dawn. Once I'd seen to all the horses, I grabbed my rope and headed to the river. On the edge of our camp sat Gabriel's small green tent. I tiptoed past, trying hard not to think of him asleep inside. It felt better to dislike him; that way things stayed simpler in my head.

Down at the river's edge a mist hung over the water. The stone bridge leading to the village curved prettily from bank to bank. It looked fairy-tale magical, a day for being brave and fighting off villains. Not that Gabriel was a villain exactly – more of a fly in my soup.

And his lack of tricks on the tightrope had given me a plan.

It took longer than usual to set up the rope. Finally, after a hot half-hour of climbing trees, I stood back to admire my handiwork. Pip gave a little high-pitched yelp. It was his way of saying he liked it too. The rope went from one bank to the other. It ran fifteen feet above the water, slightly higher on the left than the right. The distance looked about forty feet across. I'd never walked over a river before. It was a smart-looking trick indeed.

Could I do it?

The sun shone through the trees, making the river's surface twinkle like hundreds of gold sovereigns.

Could I *really* do it?

There was only one way to find out.

Spreading my shawl on the bank, I told Pip to lie down on it. He pretended not to hear, until I gave him a bread crust. 'Good boy,' I said, fussing his ears. 'Now stay right there and watch.'

I climbed the tree once more. The bark scraped my hands and bare feet. For a moment, I couldn't find the blasted rope. Then, there it was. I pulled myself into position, and inched along it. I kept one hand on the tree trunk until I found my balance.

My heart steadied. I focused up ahead. Emptied my thoughts. Now it was just me and a long, thin stretch of rope. My feet tingled. I let go of the tree and walked forwards.

A few steps out, I felt a breeze against my cheek. The rope began to sway. I bent my knees, moved my arms just a little, and kept looking forwards. Another few steps and the rope went quiet. The stillness of it made me brave. Halfway across I crouched down, dangling my leg just like Gabriel had done, and peered at the river below.

After a bit, I got to my feet, but the balance wasn't right. Gabriel had lifted one foot to steady himself; it was a tip I knew well. Doing it now, I grew still again all down my back and into my legs. When I was ready I took a step. And another.

Before I knew it I'd reached the other side.

Grinning like a lunatic I let out a great 'WHOOP!', which frightened a bird from the tree. Below on the bank, Pip blinked sleepily.

'What d'you think of that, then?' I said to him.

He yawned.

'Ta very much, Pip!'

It made me laugh, but only a bit. For it wasn't enough, not anymore. I wanted cheering and clapping and faces grinning back at me. I wanted music and fireworks. I wanted sensational headlines of the kind Blondin got. The bigger the crowd, the better.

Yet my *only* crowd so far had been Pip and Ned. And one of them was in a sulk with me. The other was half asleep.

Crossing back over the river was easy enough. My feet had the measure of the rope now. That stillness stayed strong all down my back and I felt sure I wouldn't wobble. Once I reached the middle, I walked backwards. I sat down and stood up again, and stretched out my arms and one leg like a ballerina. But when I got to the other side I didn't want to stop.

So I set off back across the rope. I went faster now, twirling my arms above my head, and turning once, twice, three times, before stepping onwards. I felt so sure, so calm. It was heaven.

Suddenly, from the riverbank, Pip started barking. Sharp manic barks they were. I tried to shut it out but he kept going. Without thinking, I turned round, too fast, too off balance. My feet slipped.

I hit the water with a thwack. One moment I was completely under, the next I'd bobbed up again like a cork. My mouth filled with water. Spluttering and cussing, I swam for the bank. What a fool I'd been to practise here. Thank heck no one had seen me.

I'd almost reached the bank when I stopped dead. At eye level I saw a pair of feet, done up in decent brown shoes. Uneasily, I looked upwards.

'Hullo Louie,' said a smart-sounding voice.

Gabriel Swift stood on the bank.

I sank back into the water. *Drat! Drat! Drat!*

There was no point in hiding; so I stood up. Jasper's old tunic stuck to me like skin. As I tugged at the fabric it made slurping noises like an animal farting. Not that Gabriel appeared to notice.

'Sorry about my cap,' he said.

'Cap? What . . . cap?'

He held up a cloth object. 'Your dog took against it.' And he *actually laughed*.

Well, it wasn't funny to me. 'Pip doesn't like strangers,' I said, which was obviously a lie since he was laying at Gabriel's feet, paws in the air as Gabriel tickled his tummy. 'Especially strangers who sneak about at the crack of dawn.'

Gabriel's hand slowed. 'It's not a crime to get up early,' he said.

Grabbing at the grass, I heaved myself out of the river. Gabriel didn't offer to help. Not that I'd have accepted it. I wanted to be as far away from him as possible.

Up on the bank, I reached for my shawl. 'Come on, you,' I said to Pip. 'We're going home.'

He shut his eyes blissfully as Gabriel carried on stroking him. It was like I didn't exist.

'Get *up*, Pip! Come on!' As I went to grab his collar Gabriel stopped me.

'You're a funambulist too,' he said, as if he'd spoken of the weather.

'And you're the *Great* Fun Ambler,' I shot back.

'Yes, but why on earth did Mr Chipchase hire me when he's already got you?'

I pulled my shawl tight around me. *Was he joking?* Something told me he wasn't, that he wanted to talk. Suddenly, it seemed, so did I.

'Those stupid do-gooders ruined my chances,' I said. 'So now Pip and me do a buffer act and we're useless. At the rate we're going I'll soon have no job at all.'

'Have you told him you can walk the tightrope?'

' 'Course I have! But he turned me down flat. Says no one wants to see children doing tricks anymore.'

'Poppycock! You'd be worth the risk.'

I glanced at him sideways. He sounded like he

meant it, but I still wasn't sure. 'But you've come from Wellbeloved's,' I said. 'They can afford to be risky.'

Gabriel's face changed. 'Wellbeloved's? That doesn't count for much.'

'It does to Mr Chipchase.'

It did to me too. Truth told, I was a bit dazzled by Wellbeloved's.

'Why?' said Gabriel. 'It's nothing special, believe me. Half the time he forgets to even pay us. It's just a bigger show, that's all.'

'Try telling Mr Chipchase. He's got this "thing" about Wellbeloved's.'

Gabriel's hand on Pip's chest went still. 'What sort of "thing"?'

I shrugged. 'He sees them as competition, I s'pose.' Though there were other big circuses out there and he never went on about them.

Gabriel didn't seem convinced either. He got to his feet. 'Perhaps I should leave,' he said. 'I don't want any trouble.'

'Bit late for that,' I said, then felt I'd been a bit unkind. 'But I'm sure you'll bring in the crowds.'

Gabriel fiddled with his cap. 'Yes. I hope so.' Then he took a deep breath. 'Well, whatever Mr Chipchase says, you are good.'

'*How* good?' I said, for I was curious despite myself.

'You've got a natural ability. Though for your next big performance, I'd leave the dog at home.'

I glared at him. 'And what big performances would those be, now you're here?'

'I wasn't mocking you, Louie. I mean it. You do have a talent.'

I dug at the ground with my toe.

'We could practise together if you like,' he said.

'What . . . you . . . and . . . me?'

'Why not? It'd help us both. Of course, if you'd rather not.'

I could think of a hundred reasons why not. Gabriel Swift had swanned into our circus and stolen my chance right from under my nose. And walking the rope with someone else was bound to be harder.

Still, I felt strangely excited.

Gabriel knew the tightrope. Lived the tightrope. Just like Blondin. Only unlike Blondin, he wasn't pictures stuck in a scrapbook. He was here in front of me, talking and breathing and wanting us to train together.

'Ask me again when I'm dry,' I said.

Quick as I could I took down the rope. Gabriel helped me hide it in the bushes. Then I whistled for

Pip. This time he came, all waggly tailed and happy. Together, we walked back towards the camp. Once we'd rounded the corner and Gabriel was out of sight, I did my own little dance for joy.

Ned was sitting on his wagon steps as I went past. He was wrapped in a blanket, drinking coffee. 'Should've woken me,' he said, then looked at my wet clothes and grinned. 'What *have* you been up to?'

So he wasn't sulking anymore. I grinned back. 'Brand new tricks.'

Ned glanced over my shoulder. His face hardened.

'What's the matter?' I said.

I turned to see Gabriel going to his tent. It did look a bit of a coincidence, us both arriving back at the showground moments apart.

'Ned,' I said in a rush. 'We were just . . .'

He spoke over me. 'I've been thinking, remember that man yesterday in the village?'

I frowned. 'What man?'

'The fancy gent in the carriage.'

'Oh, him.'

'He was looking for someone about Gabriel's age. Said the person walked the tightrope. He was offering a big reward.'

'So?'

Ned emptied his cup. 'I wonder if Mr Chipchase knows?'

'Don't be daft,' I said. 'Gabriel's a tightrope walker, not a runaway.'

'If you say so. You're the expert.'

And he got up and went inside.

CHAPTER 9

The next day we set off for the nearest big town. We'd almost reached it when Mr Chipchase had a sudden change of plan.

'Keep going till Sharpfield!' he barked. 'Drive your horses on!'

I groaned. Sharpfield was another two hours away. I'd suffered enough rough roads for one day. My very bones ached, never mind how Jasper's must be feeling.

'Why aren't we stopping?' I asked Paolo, whose wagon drew alongside ours.

'Wellbeloved's are here. Look.' He pointed to a glossy poster stuck to a wall. 'SENSATIONAL!', 'DEATH-DEFYING!', 'BLOOD-CURDLING!' it screamed. My heart skipped a beat.

Wellbeloved's.

That name was like a spell, magical and mysterious. Yet I'd never even clapped eyes on the show itself. Now, at last, we were about to drive past it. Eagerly, I sat up tall in my seat. 'So where are they?' I said, seeing nothing nearby but a churchyard and some cottages.

Up ahead, the lead wagons turned off the main road. We were now in a lane. Great hedges towered over us on either side. Any view was blotted out. We were bypassing the town altogether. I slumped down in disappointment. Then I recalled something Gabriel had said. I twisted round in my seat. 'Thought you said Wellbeloved's were in America,' I called to him. He was walking alongside our back wheel, his collar turned up so it hid most of his face.

'Mr Wellbeloved is going soon, I believe.' He was frowning again. It didn't suit him as well as a smile.

'Oh, I see.'

Except I didn't. We never ran into other shows. Two circuses in the same town at the same time was pointless. Mr Chipchase planned his stands months ahead so it wouldn't happen.

'Jasper's accident,' I said out loud. 'It's thrown our schedule, ain't it?'

'That'll be it,' Gabriel said.

Yet it didn't explain us taking the long way round. Why on earth couldn't we just ride past Wellbeloved's stand? We'd be through the town and gone again before they noticed us. What with Gabriel's change of

79

show name, done to keep Mr Wellbeloved at bay, and now this, it was like we were running away.

As we urged our tired horses into a trot, Mr Chipchase called over his shoulder. 'Louie, put a blasted hat on!'

'What for?'

He didn't hear me. Or maybe he just didn't want to answer.

*

Late afternoon we arrived in Sharpfield. The sky was dull grey, the air thick with chimney smoke. We went down streets where all the houses looked the same; row after row of grimy brickwork. On street corners children stared at us with eyes too big for their faces.

Eventually, we took a sharp turn left, through a gateway and into a factory yard. Workers on their break were leaning up against the wall.

'Showground's that way,' said a girl, pointing to another gate.

And she smiled a big, crooked teeth smile. I grinned back. Then the factory horn sounded; break was over, and she looked as grim-faced as everyone else.

I shuddered. *I could be that girl.*

If things didn't improve, I would be.

This past week Mr Chipchase had run out of patience. Tickets still weren't selling. The Great Dog Detective skit was getting worse. Even Gabriel's act lacked sparkle. Not long ago, however bad things got, I had hoped that Mr Chipchase would eventually see sense. But now even that chance was fading. He had his tightrope walker; he didn't need me.

'We're not a charity,' Mr Chipchase said after one particularly bad night.

Put plainly, if I couldn't earn my way, I'd be out. I heard it clearly behind his words. It made me sick with fear, for without the circus I had nothing. I didn't think I'd survive. It'd be like pulling a fish from the river and watching it gasp its last on the bank.

Finally, our wagons came to a halt. It was a bit grand to call it a showground. The stand itself was just half an acre of bare ground, surrounded by a wall. One by one, people jumped down from their wagons. I took off the wretched hat and scratched my head. A black cloud seemed to hang over us all.

Mr Chipchase didn't even get out of his trailer.

'Just set up!' he yelled through the window. 'We'll not be here longer than a night.' Then he noticed me. 'You! Louie! Get over here now!'

I pointed to myself. 'What? Me?'

Stupid really, there was no other Louie. No one else had been told to wear a hat either, and it now hung limp in my hands.

I climbed the steps of Mr Chipchase's wagon, expecting an earful.

'Boots!' he bellowed.

Kicking them off, I went in. Kitty sat on a low sofa. She looked at me coldly. Mr Chipchase was behind his desk, the accounts book spread open before him like a bible. I stood in front of him.

'Is this about the hat, sir? Only it itches awful and I don't see why I had to wear it.'

'What? Oh, never mind that now.'

His face looked so grave I felt myself sink. This was obviously about more than hats.

'We have a problem,' he said.

I swallowed nervously. 'Oh.'

'We're losing money. Faster than I can fathom.'

'But you've got Gabriel now,' I said. 'If anyone can bring in the crowds, he can.'

Kitty smirked. I felt myself go pink as Mr Chipchase's eyebrows shot up.

'Personally, I'm not entirely convinced by young Master Swift. It's hard to believe he comes from

Wellbeloved's, a show so notorious for its daring.'

He was right, though it did make me wince. Gabriel's routine was polished to perfection. But it wasn't exactly a sensation. It didn't have that *whiff of death* we needed to bring in the crowds.

'Anyhow, you're not here to discuss Gabriel Swift,' said Mr Chipchase.

He looked down at his accounts and grimaced. Thoughts of Jasper, our wagon and my sorry wage all rushed into my head. My heart gave a hard thump.

'Gabriel alone isn't enough to carry this show. Nor are you, Kitty,' Mr Chipchase said, knocking the smug look off her face. 'Things need to be different. Starting tonight.'

'I could do something, sir. With Gabriel, I mean,' I blurted out.

'Don't make me laugh!' said Kitty.

Mr Chipchase didn't say anything.

I glared at them both. 'It ain't funny! We're going to start practising together.'

Kitty sneered.

'If only you'd listen. We could perform together on the high wire, act out a story, that sort of thing. No one else has done it, not even Blondin.'

Mr Chipchase raised his hand for silence.

'I *can* walk the high wire! I've told you I can!' I cried. 'Ask Kitty – she's seen me.'

Most normal people would've indeed asked Kitty, whose bottom lip stuck out like a baby's. Not Mr Chipchase. He rolled his eyes skywards. 'And I've told *you* I won't allow it.'

'But Kitty knows I can do it. So does Ned, and Gabriel Swift . . .'

His fist banged down on the table so hard the pens jumped into the air. 'ENOUGH!'

I bit my lip to stop it trembling.

'As from today, the Great Dog Detective act will cease to exist.'

'You're cutting our act?' I didn't know whether to be glad or mortified.

'But she's still not earning her keep,' said Kitty. 'If she can't perform, then what's she doing here, Papa? I've often wondered.'

'That's enough, Kitty.' Mr Chipchase's voice had gone very low. He shot me a quick glance. It was enough to make me shrivel up with shame. For that look said it all: the circus might look after Jasper, who'd performed here all his life, but it couldn't carry me much longer.

Mr Chipchase came out from behind his desk,

84

pacing the small space between us. A vein bulged in his forehead. 'Listen carefully, both of you,' he said. 'I'm running out of ideas.'

In the pit of my stomach, I knew this was it. I wouldn't get another chance.

'My new plan involves you . . .' he said, stabbing at me with his finger, 'and you, Kitty.' Another stab.

I almost sank to the floor.

'Louie, you'll join Kitty's act as her assistant.'

'Please, sir!' I begged. 'Don't make me! Not an assistant! I can do so much more. If only you'd just . . .'

He cut in. 'Not just any old assistant, Louie. As from tonight, you'll stand against the board when she throws her knives. You'll be her living target.'

This had to be a joke. A very bad joke.

'A living target? But sir, think of the do-gooders! It's dangerous! The tightrope's safer by a mile!'

He wasn't listening.

'I hardly think even you can mess *this* up,' Mr Chipchase said. 'And don't worry, Kitty's very good. She never misses.'

First time for everything, I thought bitterly.

The little smile on Kitty's face said the same.

CHAPTER 10

The audience, all ten of them, stopped rustling their toffee papers. Kitty Quickblade's act was about to start. She was done up to the nines in a silver tunic tied with ribbon, which I'd sewn in place backstage. As for *my* fine costume, it was still the dung-green clown suit. And as usual my hair was plaited tightly and tucked under my hat.

'Ladies and gentlemen,' Mighty Ned boomed. 'We bring you a chilling spectacle . . . A routine where one mistake could mean instant DEATH!'

The crowd gasped.

Ned was laying it on specially thick tonight. Perhaps he'd been told to; perhaps he was still in a sulk with me. Either way, my knees shook hard. If things went wrong tonight, I'd be for it. I'd wave goodbye to any dreams of being the showstopper. Or any notions of staying here at all.

As Kitty bowed to the crowds, I did the same,

flashing my best smile till I almost began to enjoy myself.

'Get in place, weasel!' Kitty hissed when she saw what I was doing. 'And stop showing off!'

Reluctantly, I went over to the corkboard. It was round, the size of a table top. All I had to do was stand against it. Yet as Kitty faced me, my whole body started trembling. Her eyes were slits as she shifted the blade between her fingers. A cold sweat crept down my back. I tried to make myself still as a dead thing, all the while my brain screaming 'Run for your life!' Next time I'd ask for a blindfold.

Kitty raised her arm. Flicked her wrist just a fraction. The knife spun through the air. It whizzed past my left ear and went *thwunk* into the board behind me. I breathed again, though I'd barely drawn air when a second knife went *whoosh* past my right side. A ringing filled my ears. The blade, still quivering, tickled my cheek. Now I couldn't move my head.

Zip. Another knife skimmed my left elbow. Then the same on my right side. I twitched in alarm. Kitty took aim, tipped her hand. A glint of steel, then *thwack thud* as the final knives hit the board either side of my legs. The spectators clapped half-heartedly.

Kitty turned to the crowd. Mighty Ned started speaking. I supposed this was my cue to move but I couldn't. The knives snagged my sleeves and trouser legs, leaving me pinned like a butterfly in a glass case. I tried wriggling my arms, then . . .

Thwack thud.

My heart stopped. Directly above my head a new knife stuck out of the board. I glared at Kitty, who gave me a nasty little wink. This time the audience clapped with gusto. Kitty bowed to the crowd. Then she turned and tried to tell me something with her eyes.

'What?' I mouthed.

She nodded furiously. A snigger went through the audience. She 'shooed' with her hands at the board behind me. Then I realised: she wanted her knives back.

My entire outline was marked out by daggers. A couple of sharp yanks freed my arms. Reaching up, I grabbed the other knives. Most came out easy enough, though my trouser leg tore. But the final blade had caught in my hair. Across the ring, Kitty eyed me coldly. People began talking and shifting in their seats. Try as I might, the knife wouldn't budge.

Screwing up my eyes, I jerked forwards. The pain was fierce, the ripping sound even worse. Then I was free. A great hunk of hair hung from the knife. The crowd cheered and clapped like mad things. It beat the sound of being scalped alive any day of the week.

Clearly Kitty didn't think so. Crossing the ring, she looked ready to thrash me. 'Get that last knife out! Quickly!'

She tried distracting the crowd but by now they were cheering for a different kind of act.

'Swap over, why don't you?' A man shouted out. 'Let the red-haired lassie do the throwing, and the dark one take the brunt.'

'Too right!' yelled someone else. 'Poor girl. It ain't fair she gets to risk life and limb. I'd rather it was t'other way round.'

More laughing and jeering. I didn't dare look at Kitty. And that stupid knife of hers still wouldn't come free. Bracing myself, I heaved and heaved. But the damned thing stayed bedded up to its hilt.

Her face appeared right next to mine. 'You're useless, weasel.'

I despised her more than ever. Gripping the knife one last time, I imagined it was her neck. At last, with a kissing sound, it slid free.

Kitty wrenched it from my hand. As she did so her eyes went wide in surprise. The crowd gave an enormous jeer, as she spun round, arms flailing. A small white dog was swinging from her tunic.

'Get him off me!' she screamed.

Where Pip had come from, I didn't know. He certainly wasn't part of the act.

Now he wriggled and thrashed like a fish on a hook. He wouldn't let go. I knew I should stop him, but I couldn't quite move.

'Get him off me!' Twisting round, Kitty tried to grab Pip. I got to him first. His little body was all tight and bristling. I wasn't sure I could hold him.

Then Mighty Ned's voice filled the tent. 'John Robinson, please come to the exit.'

It was the name no artist wanted to hear. It meant the act had gone so far wrong it had to be halted. The band struck up a tune, the lights brightened. Kitty stormed out of the ring, her tunic in tatters. Pip and me followed at a distance. The very thing I'd feared had happened; now I felt sick with dread.

Backstage, Ned gripped my shoulders and peered into my face. 'What's got into you, Louie?'

'I . . . I . . . I don't know.' I was too embarrassed to meet his eye.

'Well, you've run out of chances,' he said, as if this was news to me.

The clowns and Rosa looked on awkwardly. There was no sign of Gabriel, which was a small relief. But still I wanted to curl up and hide. For my shame was their shame; one bad performance affected us all.

'You were stealing the show with all that smiling and bowing,' Ned said.

I shrugged. I'd enjoyed the crowd, they'd enjoyed me. Yet that was now a crime too, apparently.

'And getting Pip to attack Kitty? That's a low blow, Louie.'

'I didn't make him do it!'

Ned gave me an 'I don't believe you' look. Tears sprang in my eyes. Why the heck was Ned siding with Kitty all of a sudden? I buried my face in Pip's fur. There didn't seem much left to say.

'I'm going to put some proper clothes on,' I said.

Once I'd changed out of the clown suit I thought I'd feel better. But even in my own frock with my hair loose again I still felt awful. Ned was right. And so was Kitty. I'd done myself no favours tonight.

Just as I was about to slope off, the backstage curtains flew open. Mr Chipchase came marching towards me.

'What the devil!' he bellowed. 'Do you mean to ruin this circus, once and for all?'

Kitty was right behind him.

I shuddered. Mr Chipchase had given me another chance and I'd thrown it away. There was nothing I could say. I turned and made for the side of the tent. Pip raced ahead of me.

'COME HERE THIS INSTANT!' Mr Chipchase yelled.

I didn't look back. Ducking under the canvas, I ran out into the night.

Halfway across the showground I slowed to a jog, unsure what I was doing or where I was going. I couldn't go home. It'd be the first place they'd look for me. And Jasper had to be spared.

Pulling Pip to me, I hid behind the nearest tent. My heartbeat began to slow.

Then came footsteps.

Shadows fell across the grass. I held my breath and put a hand over Pip's muzzle to stop him barking. Two figures approached. One was tallish, wearing a ringmaster's hat. The other was squat like a toad.

'I've let this go on too long,' Mr Chipchase said.

'But Louie's marvellous,' said Ned. 'If you saw her, you might change your mind.'

'That girl's had every sort of chance!'

'Not this chance, sir. And what with Gabriel Swift

not being quite so special with his tricks . . .' Ned stopped, letting it hang in the air.

Mr Chipchase didn't reply. But I groaned silently, begging Ned to shut up.

'See, sir,' said Ned, 'I've a notion someone is after Gabriel, someone who wants to find him quite badly. This man has a carriage, and money by the look of him. It won't be long before he tracks us down.'

I cussed under my breath. Trust Ned to stick his nose in. All this talk about a man in a carriage was just gossip. It had a touch of sour grapes about it too. It wasn't fair to take things out on Gabriel. Ned was just stirring up trouble.

'Is that so?' said Mr Chipchase.

'If Gabriel goes, you'll need a showstopper again, won't you, sir?'

'Yes,' said Mr Chipchase. 'And it won't be Louie, mark my words.'

The shadows moved on.

It was too much to take in. I took a belly-deep gulp of air and, bit by bit, my mind cleared. So it was final. No showstopper chances for me. Ever. Sorry though I was for Gabriel, I felt sorrier for myself. My own mother hadn't wanted me. And now the circus didn't want me either.

It was time to leave.

My first thought was Jasper. He'd insist on coming with me, which was the very worst idea. He could hardly stand upright, let alone do a day's work out in the big wide world. Staying here, he had a home at least. It was all anyone could hope for right now.

I decided to go quickly. Tonight, and not tell anyone. It was best that way. There'd be no goodbyes, no lingering glances. I'd not even take Pip. He'd be better off here with food and a warm bed, and Jasper, who'd need the company.

Dear Pip.

Oh heck. My chin trembled. *Could I do it? Could I leave all this behind?*

I looked down at my dog. 'Go home, little man.'

He cocked his head at me but didn't shift from my side.

'Go home, Pip! Find Jasper!' I pointed in the direction of our wagon.

He licked his lips but still wouldn't budge.

'Just go, you rotten dog! Go!' I cried.

Pip's ears went down. He looked up at me with huge wet eyes, then slid off into the darkness. I started to sob uncontrollably. My mam, I'd bet, was made of tougher stuff. She'd left me without a backwards glance.

CHAPTER 11

Hiding here wouldn't solve things. Before I'd moved a step, the tent opened and a figure appeared.

'Why don't you come in?'

The voice was velvet deep. It belonged to Miss Lilly.

I swear my own feet defied me, and before I knew it, I was inside her tent. On an old chest in the corner a lamp burned low. There was just enough light to see Miss Lilly. She wore her usual loose-fitting white dress. Her hair stood out wild from her head.

'I should go,' I said, wiping away my tears. 'Mr Chipchase is after me.'

Her face was in shadow. Prickles ran up and down my neck.

'Sit,' she said.

Bracelets tinkled down her arm as she waved to her left. I sank into a seat full of cushions.

Miss Lilly scooped back her hair. Twisting it in a knot against her neck, she then lit more lamps. Except these weren't normal lamps; these were fancy things made of coloured glass that glittered reds and blues and purples, making the room seem strewn with jewels. There were scarves hanging from the roof and more cushions scattered about the floor. The air smelled sweet, like spices, as though I'd walked into a scene from the Arabian Nights itself. Slowly, gently, I began to relax.

Miss Lilly slid into the seat opposite. A small table stood between us; underneath it her knees bumped against mine. I jerked back in my seat.

'I won't hurt you, child,' she said. 'No more than you're hurting yourself.'

I frowned. 'What do you mean?'

'Your life is difficult. You face choices – about your past and your future.'

My fingers clenched and unclenched. I didn't want to talk. This was best left inside my head. Looking up, I met Miss Lilly's gaze. Her eyes were so dark there was no telling their colour. I didn't want this strangeness. It belonged in Miss Lilly's world. All I wanted was to live with Jasper and Pip, and be part of the circus. Now it seemed even that was too much to ask for.

'Perhaps the cards hold the answers to your problems,' she said.

'No, ta,' I said, shifting uneasily. 'Not a reading. Not tonight.'

But Miss Lilly had already placed a cloth-wrapped bundle on the table. She shook out her hands as if she'd just washed them. Ever so slowly, she peeled back the cloth. I watched, nervously at first, then I felt myself being drawn in.

Beneath the cloth was Miss Lilly's tarot deck. Face down they looked like normal cards, curled at the corners and with a dark swirly pattern on their backs.

'Take them,' Miss Lilly instructed.

I wiped my hands on my skirts, for my palms were sweating. As I picked up the cards, a tingling spread up my arm.

'Ask them what you want to know.'

I drew a breath to speak but Miss Lilly cut in. 'Don't say it out loud. Say it in your head.'

So I did.

I handed the cards back to her. She shut her eyes and her lips moved silently. When she opened her eyes again, they were pools of black. She dealt the cards quickly, laying one on top of another in the centre of the table. Around them, she placed four more. Then down the right-hand side, she laid out a final four cards. These were all face down. The others were face up.

'Are you ready?' she said.

I swallowed. 'Ready as I'll ever be.'

Miss Lilly reached for the centre card and held it towards me. The picture was of a man with a knapsack, stepping off a cliff top.

'The fool,' she said.

'Huh,' I slouched back in my seat. 'Might've guessed *that* one. Louie Reynolds: the great big idiot.'

'That's not what it means,' said Miss Lilly.

'Oh?'

'It means you are young and naïve, but that adventure awaits you.'

I sat forward.

'But,' Miss Lilly raised her finger in warning, 'you must choose the right path.'

Easier said than done. I sat back again.

The next card lay at right angles to the first. Miss Lilly peered at it. Her mouth twitched.

'It's bad, ain't it?' I said.

'This card is your obstacle.' She showed me. On it was a dark shape with leering eyes, standing over a woman. 'The devil.'

I shivered. 'Which means evil, surely?'

'In a way. It means you're miserable, and you're suffering.'

My heart filled up with Jasper and Pip, and how I wanted to be a showstopper so much it hurt. 'Yes.' I bit back tears. 'That does fit well.'

The next card was at Miss Lilly's twelve o'clock. Her gaze swept over it, then she turned it so I could see too. 'Your goal,' she said. 'The wheel of fortune.'

The card showed a yellow cartwheel spinning towards a cliff edge. *Cliffs again.* It was a good job I wasn't scared of heights.

'This is your destiny card. Your fortune.'

I laughed hotly. '*My* fortune? *My* luck? It's bleeding lousy. I don't need a card to tell me that.'

I got up.

'No,' she said, pulling me down again. 'You must see all the cards, otherwise your reading is incomplete.'

I tried to shrug her off. 'I have to get going, Miss Lilly. I've been here long enough.'

But she held me firm. 'Stay,' she said.

So I stayed, fidgeting nervously in my seat. It was flimflam really, this tarot lark. And any time now Mr Chipchase would find me here.

Miss Lilly took another card. Turning it over, her face suddenly darkened.

'The tower.'

The way she said it made me more uneasy.

'Your past,' she said, and pushed the card towards me.

But I couldn't seem to look at it, gazing instead at Miss Lilly and wondering why her eyes shone with tears.

'You must look,' she said gently. 'You must face your past.'

My heart began to pound.

My past.

Two words that made me clench up inside. That made me hurt for the mother who hadn't wanted me. Who'd left me at the circus and had never come back.

Miss Lilly tapped the card with her finger. In my head, I counted to three, then I looked down. It was a picture of a tower crumbling to pieces as lightning hit it. In among the flying bricks a body tumbled to the ground.

I felt suddenly strange. My head filled up with a whirling, rushing noise. I grabbed the table to steady myself.

'Gently now, Louie,' said Miss Lilly. 'You've had a reaction to the card, that's all.'

'Please,' I said. 'I have to go.'

'But we must finish your tarot reading. We will look

to the future and find out what's to become of you, my dear.'

She reached for a card. Then stopped. Outside the tent came a rustling sound – boots striding through grass. Her eyes locked with mine.

Someone was out there.

A shadow, *two shadows*, loomed across the canvas. I leaped to my feet. Too fast, too quick, for I almost lifted the table clean off the floor.

'Your cards!' Miss Lilly cried as they slid into her lap.

One card fell to the floor. It lay there, picture side up. I dearly wished I'd not seen it. My blood turned cold.

'That's my future, is it?'

Miss Lilly hesitated.

'*Is it?*'

'Yes,' she said.

The picture was of a skeleton, the word 'DEATH' in big letters above it. Then two voices came from outside the tent.

First was Kitty: 'She's in there. I can hear her.'

Then Mr Chipchase: 'Leave this to me.'

Miss Lilly was trying to tell me something. She pointed to the DEATH card on the floor and held up another with stars on it. I wasn't listening. I had to get out of here. But how? The walls of the tent all looked the same.

'Where's the door?' I hissed.

Miss Lilly pointed right at the spot where the shadows stood. I was cornered. There was nowhere to run.

The tent flew open. Two figures barged in, their lanterns blinding me.

'Stay where you are!' said Mr Chipchase.

Not likely.

I dodged him, ploughing straight into Kitty. Her hands snatched my hair and my head jerked back. I kicked out like a horse, landing a cracking blow on her shin.

'You little bleeder!' She let go of me as if I was poker-hot.

I ran for the showground gates.

CHAPTER 12

The main road into Sharpfield was hectic busy. Coach lamps and hoof beats whizzed by in the darkness. It was a miracle I didn't get trampled flat. Not that I cared. I was sobbing so much I feared I'd never stop. The best thing was to keep walking. Each step put the circus further behind me.

Eventually, I found myself in the main part of town. My face was wet with tears and snot. Since my own show had been cut short, it was still quite early. And this pesky road was still mighty busy. By now I'd reached another of those streets where all the houses looked the same. Gas lamps gave off just enough light for me to see I wasn't alone. Clusters of people in their best coats and hats were heading up the hill. They seemed in high spirits. Despite my own wretchedness I was curious, and fell in beside a man and his missus.

'Where you all going at this hour?' I asked.

The man and the woman shared a little excited glance.

'Haven't you heard?' he said.

The woman chipped in. 'Where've you been, duckie?'

With a stupid circus, I thought bitterly.

The woman seemed to take pity on me, sore-eyed and mud-splattered as I was. She rummaged in her purse and pulled out a handbill.

'Here. Keep it, if you like.'

So much for us coming to Sharpfield, then; there was another show here tonight too. It explained why so few punters had come to ours. Opening the handbill, I braced myself to see what big attraction had trumped our dog and pony show.

I read the words once. Twice. My heart stopped still. And then it was pounding so fast again that I could only gasp.

Great snakes alive! Could it be true? Could this really be happening? Here, tonight?

I read the handbill a third time.

'MARVELLOUS! MARVELLOUS! MARVEL-LOUS!' it said. 'FOR ONE NIGHT ONLY...'

One word stood out bigger than the rest. That word, *that name*, was as familiar to me as my own.

How many times had I read it, cut it out of newspapers, posters, seen it in bright lights inside my head?

BLONDIN.

The Great Blondin.

My Blondin.

Call him what you want – he was here! Tonight!

All my bad luck, and now . . . *this*. A heaven-sent slice of good fortune. I wasn't going to miss it for the world.

The venue was easy to find since half of England was heading for it. Just off the market place was a splendid building with pillars outside. It looked like a theatre. The front steps teemed with people, all chattering and clutching their tickets as if they were the crown jewels themselves.

I faltered; I didn't have a ticket. And I'd bet in a place as grand as this there'd be someone checking. Even our little circus did that.

Sure enough, men in flat caps moved among the crowds.

'Get yer tickets ready! No ticket? Then no joy tonight, ladies and gents.'

And they meant it too. One chap got yanked from the steps before my very eyes.

'Don't try it again!' the flat cap hollered, kicking the man's backside halfway up the street.

There had to be some other way of getting in. Directly opposite the theatre were food stalls, selling coffee and meat pies and hot potatoes. The smells made my stomach growl. I ducked behind the pie stall. And waited.

Eventually, the last of the punters went inside. The flat caps followed. I'd have to move fast. At any moment, the performance would be starting, and I wasn't going to miss a second of it.

Far as I could tell there was only one way into the theatre: the main doorway, which was now shut. Through the steamed-up glass, shapes moved backwards and forwards. Flat caps, I bet, and ticket girls. I'd never get past them. Not a chance.

I wracked my brains. There had to be a way in around the back. A cellar, a side window left open. *Something! Anything!* If only Ned was here. He'd have worked it out with me or stood by as lookout. This time it was down to me alone. And it made my head hurt, for the theatre was connected on both sides by more buildings. There really was no other way in.

One thing was certain; I couldn't just stand here,

not with Blondin a stone's throw away across the street.

A hand came down on my shoulder.

'Take this over there will you, girl?' said a man's voice. 'There's a penny in it for you if you do.'

I spun round to see the pie seller handing me two steaming pies wrapped in paper. He nodded towards the theatre.

I didn't need telling twice. Swiping the pies from him, I raced across the road and up the steps. A nudge of the elbow and the glass door swung open. I stepped into a brightly lit hallway. Two girls sat counting tickets behind a desk, their faces thick with rouge. The flat caps stood at the foot of a red-carpeted staircase. They all eyed me coldly.

'Pies!' I said, holding the hot bundle aloft.

'Are they for me?' said a flat cap.

' 'Course they are, dimwit,' said one of the ticket girls. 'No one else ordered 'em.'

I placed the paper-wrapped parcel on the desk in front of her. The smell of gravy wafted out and the girl wrinkled her nose. 'Ugh, it stinks. Take it somewhere else, Harry.'

Harry came over to claim his pies. And as he did so his mates started ragging him, saying he had to share them and really he was a cheapskate to have only ordered two. They bickered and jostled in front of the girls. They'd forgotten I was even there.

This was my chance.

Tiptoeing past the desk, I took the stairs two at a time. No one came after me. It was almost too easy. At the top of the stairs was a corridor. At its end was a pair of double doors. I could hear the crowd beyond them, a whistling, thrumming sound that made me shiver.

Suddenly, a man behind me shouted, 'Oi! You! Come back here!'

I started to run, praying those double doors would open.

'Stop! You!'

He was gaining on me. *Just ten more yards to the doors.* From inside the theatre came clapping and cheering. I willed my legs to go faster. Grabbing for the handle, I smelled meat gravy. Harry the flat cap was right behind me, still carrying his pies. With his free hand he seized my skirts.

'Got you, you little toe-rag!'

He yanked me backwards, all the while holding his pies out of harm's way as I fought like a ferret in a sack. My frock ripped. He still held on. I had a firm grip on the door handle now. As he pulled me back the door inched open. Through the tiniest sliver I saw dazzling lights and row upon row of punters. I gasped in wonder.

Yet this Harry cove wouldn't give up. I stopped wriggling till his hold eased. Then, swinging my arm, I elbowed him hard. His pies were now a big splatty mess on the carpet. His nose didn't look pretty either.

'I'll have you, you little . . .'

As he lunged for me again I sidestepped through the doors.

Once inside, I didn't hang about. There were punters everywhere: sitting down, standing up, lining the aisles, squeezed into the balcony. The place stank of gas jets and damp overcoats and unwashed hair. It was hot as hell. And the excitement was so sharp I could taste it.

I elbowed my way right down to the front of the balcony. The crowd swallowed me up. That flat cap would never find me now. Below in the stalls, there were hundreds more punters. Great lamps blazed from the gilded walls. Red drapes hung across the stage and at every entrance. It was a rum sight indeed.

Then I saw Gabriel Swift.

He stood only a few feet away from me. And like everyone else, he looked flushed with heat and excitement. Reaching out, I grabbed his sleeve.

'You knew about this and didn't tell me?'

He jumped out of his skin. 'Gosh, Louie, don't do that!' he cried.

I squeezed in beside him. As our shoulders bumped I swore he was trembling. It dawned on me then that maybe he'd run away too. Perhaps Mr Chipchase had had words. Told him his act wasn't daring enough. It was wrong to feel it, but it did make things better. At least I wasn't on my own anymore.

'Don't worry,' I said, 'Mr Chipchase won't come after us.'

'Mr Chipchase? Why would he do that?' Gabriel said, surprised.

'You've run away, haven't you?'

He looked taken aback. 'No . . . at least not . . . well, I've just come for the show.'

'Oh.' I felt stupid. So I was on my own after all.

'I did try to find you, Louie. You see, I overheard a fellow from the factory talking about *this* show. I came looking for you straight away.'

'You did?'

He nodded. 'Anyone serious about the tightrope admires Blondin, am I right?'

He was. Dead right.

'I've kept a scrapbook on him for years,' I said. 'There ain't much I don't know about Blondin.' It came out a bit wrong, making me sound like a show-off. But it was the first time I'd admitted it to anyone.

Gabriel sounded impressed. 'Gosh, no wonder your technique is so advanced.'

'You think?' I felt better hearing this.

'Oh yes. I bought us both tickets, you know.'

'Who needs tickets?'

He stared at me in awe. 'You got in here without a ticket?'

Clearly it hadn't occurred to him to do the same.

At that moment, the lights dipped. A master of ceremonies took to the stage. 'Tonight, good citizens of Sharpfield, we have a very special performer . . .'

High in the roof space was a length of rope, running from one side of the theatre to the other. A curtained-off platform was up there too, and from it a figure now appeared.

Straight away I knew it was him. With his dark pointy beard and flesh-coloured tights he looked just like he did in the papers. Even so, it took a moment for my eyes and brain to connect.

It was Blondin. *My* Blondin.

He was here, in the same place as me, breathing the same too-warm air. It was a job not to swoon on the spot. But what a waste that would be, to faint away and miss the whole thing! Later, I'd go over it all in my head, right down to the smallest details. Now, I simply gazed. And forgot everything else.

Blondin bowed for the crowds.

'Same rope he used at Niagara, so they say,' said Gabriel.

Niagara. It sounded like a magic word and made me shudder in delight. I thought of all my scrapbook clippings, of Blondin dwarfed by the river beneath. What nerve he had! What daring! The only river I'd tried to cross I'd gone belly up into. I could only dream of having his skills.

Now Blondin stepped onto the rope. I leaned forward, elbows on the balcony rail. In real life, he didn't look *quite* the same as in his pictures. He was rounder at the chest, with narrow legs and a drooping set of whiskers at his mouth. He looked smaller somehow, and a bit . . . well . . . *old*.

Yet with his very first step – *oh goodness alive* – my botherings vanished. He moved like a bird. His feet took little fairy steps. Every movement was so easy, so natural he might've been walking on air.

Just as my brain got used to it, when I was sure he was safe, Blondin stood stock still. He lay down flat on the rope and rolled right over so he was face down, waving to the crowd below. I watched in amazement. He even did swimming strokes, kicking his feet and flailing his arms. All around me people 'ooohed' and 'aaahed', and I clapped till my palms stung. Then he got up again and started walking, taking huge, silly, clownish strides and we all laughed and cheered him along his way. It was sheer pantomime. I'd never seen high-wire walking like it.

Once, he even pretended to fall. The crowd gasped. A woman near me clutched her husband. My own stomach leaped to my throat. But the Great Blondin righted himself just in time. He finished with a backflip somersault.

A somersault on the high wire!

I could hardly believe my eyes. It brought the house down. Jumping for sheer joy, I whooped myself hoarse.

There was no denying it; Blondin was the best. Gabriel Swift might look better close up, but he didn't do any tricks. And this was what the crowd wanted. Blondin had them eating out of his hand.

After Blondin came the fire-eaters and a man with

a talking crow. Then there was a woman who could fold herself in half and fit inside an apple crate. The crowd clapped politely. But we were saving our cheers for Blondin, who we knew would return for his finale.

The lights went up. It was interval time. And Gabriel and me were suddenly talking all at once.

'He was brilliant, wasn't he?' I cried.

'He was. It was genius!'

'The way he swam along the rope!'

'And when he nearly fell!'

As the crowd surged around us we babbled on and on. Gabriel was all lit up with it. He looked different, less cagey. It was like seeing the real person for the first time. I bet it was all there in my face too, the sheer joy of finding someone who understood Blondin. Who loved the tightrope like I did.

Then, right by us, the crowd moved apart. Gabriel's face suddenly froze.

'Oh no,' he said, and stepped backwards.

The crowd started jostling. There were catcalls and sharp elbows. It was hard to stay upright. Quickly, I lost sight of Gabriel. Standing on tiptoe, I strained to see over people's heads.

'Gabriel!' I yelled. 'Gabriel!' But there was no sign of him.

The crowd closed in again. The lights dimmed and the music started up. I squeezed back into my place at the balcony rail. But the excitement had gone. I was more bothered about Gabriel, who'd vanished into thin air. It wasn't the same watching Blondin without him.

Yet I wasn't without company for long. A dandy-looking gent parked himself slap bang in front of me. He was wearing the most stupidly tall top hat.

'Excuse me, mister,' I said, for I now couldn't see a thing.

The man ignored me. He was looking up at the platform, where Blondin was about to reappear.

I tapped him on the shoulder. 'Mister. Your hat.'

He didn't turn round. I tapped harder, irritated. Any minute now the show would be starting again and there was no other space to stand.

'Oi! Mister! Your hat's like a blinking church spire, and I can't see round it!'

The man shuddered. He turned ever so slowly, as if he was about to cuff me round the ear. I braced myself. Yet seeing me, his eyes went saucer-wide. He stared for a very long moment. It made me chill, like someone had walked over my grave. Then he touched the brim of his hat, just once, and moved on through the crowd.

CHAPTER 13

Now I'd got my view back, I wasn't budging for anyone. The finale was starting.

A blue painted wheelbarrow emerged from behind the curtains on the platform. Blondin had done it before, of course. I'd seen the headlines: 'HERO OF NIAGARA PUSHES LIVE LION IN WHEEL-BARROW.' It was madness. I only hoped Gabriel was still watching.

Up on his platform, Blondin waved with one hand. He then took the barrow's handles. Pushing it forwards, the little front wheel trundled along the rope. Then Blondin was on the rope too, stepping lightly, neatly as ever. I gripped the balcony rail, heart in mouth. The whole theatre fell silent.

Any second the lion would appear . . .

Blondin and his wheelbarrow were now halfway across the rope. But still no lion had shown itself. I began to wonder if it had fallen asleep, or if it had died of fright, poor brute. For I confess, I did feel a little sorry for it.

Blondin leaned forward. He seemed to be speaking to something inside the wheelbarrow. He looked vexed. He'd even let go of one handle and was pointing his finger in a telling-off way. As if by magic, a child's head peeped out. I blinked. Stared again. *Definitely a child.*

The whole theatre drew breath together. It wasn't a happy sound.

Gripping the sides of the barrow, the child moved into a crouching position. She stood with agonising slowness. Or almost stood, for she wouldn't let go of the sides. She was a dear little thing; I'd have guessed about six years old. A crown of flowers sat lopsided in her hair. And her face was white with fear.

A lion I could just about stomach. But even for me, raised in the circus, this was too much.

'Great heavens! Poor mite!' said a woman next to me. 'I've not got the nerves to watch *this*.'

I had to agree.

Slowly, the wheelbarrow trundled forwards. Blondin spoke to the child again. This time she let go with one hand and waved to the crowd. Few people waved back. Bending stiffly, she scooped something up from the bottom of the barrow. She stood with a fistful of rose petals, which fell through her fingers like snow.

The petals were a pretty distraction at first, and the girl herself almost smiled. Then she wobbled. Her arms flailed. As she sat down with a bump, the barrow lurched sideways. The entire theatre groaned. I was sure the whole lot would go crashing to the ground. Then miraculously the barrow righted itself and the crowd went 'aaah' in relief. Even Blondin managed a shaky grin. I felt sick. The only sign of the girl now was a tiny hand, still gripping onto the side. It was pitiful.

'She's his own daughter, apparently,' said the same woman. 'What kind of parent would do that to their own flesh and blood?'

I shook my head. I didn't know. Or maybe I did, for an ache had started under my ribs. I glanced about for Gabriel, but still couldn't see him. The crowd was growing more unsettled. There were tuttings and murmurings. Some people began to leave.

Then behind me a man started cursing. 'That blasted devil! How dare he? How DARE he?'

I turned. The gent in the too-tall top hat stood just a few feet away. He was waving his fist and staring upwards.

'Has he no shame?' he went on. 'Has he not a single, solitary idea of his own?'

The rant seemed directed at Blondin. Or rather the empty tightrope above our heads, for Blondin had made a sharp exit himself.

This man was mad, I decided, as people scurried past us. There was space around him now, and for the first time I got a good look at him. His clothes were dark like a towner's, and yet he wasn't a towner, not quite. His cravat was too bright, his shirt cuffs a bit too fancy. And his side whiskers weren't the normal mutton-chop kind but groomed into sharp points along his jawbone.

He caught me staring. His fist fell to his side. 'Good evening,' he said, touching his hat. 'Did you like the show?'

His eyes were a strange, silver shade. They made me rather flustered. 'Yes . . . I mean . . . no.'

'An interesting answer,' he said.

He had an air about him. *Like a man who knew his business*, I thought with a shiver, *whatever business that might be.* The crowd jostled us apart and I lost sight of him. I was glad of it too.

*

Back outside, the street was busy with carriages and people saying their farewells. There was still no Gabriel. I asked a few punters if they'd seen a blond-haired lad in a dark suit. But it wasn't much help. A crowd this size held many such boys and not one of them was Gabriel. Then, all too quickly, the last of the carriages left and the street fell quiet. It started to rain. A sinking feeling took hold of me. I needed a plan. *Just don't think of home*, I told myself.

First thing to find was a doorway to sleep in. I set off in the direction the carriages had gone. It brought me into the town square. Tall buildings loomed dark on all sides, throwing their shadows across the cobbles. It was as quiet as the dead here. Not the sort of place I fancied spending the night. I hurried on.

Out of nowhere came a rumbling sound. It got louder. Closer. There were hoofbeats too. Turning, I saw the lamps of an approaching carriage. The horses drew alongside me and a window slid down.

'Have you no home to go to, young lady?'

Without even looking, I knew who it was. The gent's voice was like his clothes; almost a rich towner's, but not quite. My heart thudded against my ribs. 'I'm on my way,' I lied.

'Then can I offer you a lift?'

I had wits enough not to get into a stranger's carriage.

'My mam's expecting me,' I said, 'and she'll wallop me one if I'm late.'

'Really?' said the top-hatted man, like this was a private joke. 'How fortunate you are to have such a caring mother.'

I shot him a glance. His face with its sharp side whiskers seemed to hover beside me. The uneasiness spread to my stomach.

Soon as a side alley appeared I ducked down it. I heard the carriage stop, the man call out. I broke into a run. The alley led into a narrow court so dark I couldn't see where I was treading, though the stench was terrible enough. I stood flat against a wall, hardly daring to breathe. The man didn't follow me. Eventually, the carriage moved on. I waited a bit longer to be safe, then went back out to the street.

The rain was falling steadily now. My head ached and the sinking feeling came back stronger. *Don't think of home*, I reminded myself. *Think of anything but home.*

There were no doorways to sleep in, just walls and gates bolted shut. I kept walking. Walking. *And don't think of top-hatted men.* It wasn't much of a choice, being heartbroken or scared silly. My thoughts turned to Blondin. Only that wasn't much comfort either. I felt totally bewildered, as if someone had told me the sky was actually green. Blondin was my hero. Had always been my hero. All these years, I'd followed his every step.

Now all I saw was his daughter's fingers gripping that wheelbarrow. She'd been terrified. It just wasn't right. Parents were meant to protect their children. That was how it worked. Or was supposed to work. It hadn't been like that for me.

One thing I did know; my dream to walk the high wire was fast becoming a nightmare. Even Blondin, it turned out, wasn't so 'great' after all. Maybe it was time to wake up. But to what? Walking the high wire was all I had. Abandon the dream and I was a nobody. A nobody whose own mother didn't even want her.

By now I felt too exhausted even for tears. My frock was soaked through and my hair stuck like rat's tails to my face. All I wanted was to lie down and sleep. Up ahead was a shop selling eyeglasses. A covered doorway fronted the street; I made for it like it was the Ritz itself. The door had a big advert on it: 'SEE EVERYTHING!' it said above a picture of a dog wearing glasses. The dog was white like Pip, and it made me get a lump in my throat. I'd seen too much tonight. I didn't want to *see* any more.

*

I must've dozed off in the doorway. Next thing, I heard footsteps. I sat bolt upright. It was that man in the top hat, I knew it. Heart pounding, I shrank back into the doorway and got ready to bite, kick, whatever it might take.

A pair of enormous feet stopped right in front of me. I'd have known them anywhere. I almost laughed with relief. 'What you doing here, Ned?'

'Gabriel reckoned I'd find you in town. Said he'd seen you at Blondin's show.' He peered into the gloomy doorway. 'Why you sleeping here?'

So Gabriel hadn't run off. He'd gone home, and I'd never see him again. I tried hard to think of something else.

'What d'you want, Ned?' I said.

He laughed. 'Ain't you going to invite me in?'

'Not funny.'

'Come on, then.' Taking my arm he tried to pull me upright.

'I ain't going anywhere.'

He must've caught sight of my face in the gaslight, for this time his laugh sounded strained. 'Come on, Louie. Don't muck about.'

As he tugged at me again my nerves snapped. 'For pity's sake, don't you get it? I ain't mucking about. I ain't going back to Chipchase's!'

And I started to cry in big messy sobs. Ned ducked into the doorway and crouched beside me. I wiped my face and got to my feet.

'There's no place for me at the circus anymore. You saw me tonight. I was useless. I'm ruining it for everybody.'

'You're doing better than some.'

He meant Gabriel, of course. 'Save your bad mouthing, Ned. You're just making trouble. And why on earth did you tell Mr Chipchase about that man asking questions?'

'How did you know about that?' he said, looking shifty.

'I heard you, you great clot.'

'Well, Mr Chipchase was mighty interested.'

'But it's just stupid gossip!'

'You don't know that,' said Ned, so smug I wanted to scream.

I tried to push past him but he blocked the doorway.

'Get out of my way.'

He didn't move.

'I'm warning you, Ned Bailey, I'll thump you if I have to.'

He sighed wearily. 'Mr Chipchase sent me to find you. He wants to speak to you.'

'Don't talk daft.'

'It's true.'

'And what does he want me for?' I snorted. 'To be Kitty's living target again?'

'He's actually been worried about you,' said Ned. 'Word is he didn't even touch his supper.'

'Shock! Horror!' I said, for Mr Chipchase had the appetite of a giant. He was forever popping buttons off his waistcoats that muggins here had to sew back on.

'Well, I'm not going back there. I'm decided,' I said.

Ned folded his arms. 'Is that so?'

Minutes later, I was eating my words.

CHAPTER 14

Back at the showground, we went straight to Mr Chipchase's caravan. I'd turned into a great knot of nerves. Before I could even think clearly, the door swung open. Gabriel appeared in a pool of light.

'You'd better come in,' he said.

I was dying to ask why he'd scarpered off so quick, and to tell him all about Blondin's poor little daughter. But he'd already taken my arm and was guiding me inside.

'I'll be off, then,' Ned said, and went without saying goodnight.

This time I wasn't asked to take my boots off; I trod mud into the carpet and was offered the very best chair. Kitty wouldn't look at me. She sat in a corner, her eyes puffed like she'd been crying.

'Louie, my dear,' Mr Chipchase said, perching his ample backside on the desk.

I frowned. *My dear?* This was getting stranger by the minute.

'There was a . . .' he searched for the word, '. . . *misunderstanding* . . . this evening. It seems you do indeed have a talent this circus needs.'

I glanced at Gabriel. He smiled in a way that didn't reach his eyes.

'I do have a talent, sir, yes,' I said, thinking how I'd tried to tell Mr Chipchase this myself. 'But you weren't interested.'

'Let's just say I've been convinced,' he said, tapping the side of his nose.

'By Ned and his gossip? Because I really don't see the link.'

He laughed a bit too loudly. 'Good gracious, no! Whatever gave you that idea?'

'Well, sir, this evening you were all for getting rid of me.'

'Nonsense, nonsense! This is your home, Louie.'

I was mightily confused. 'But, sir, didn't you . . .'

I trailed off. Had Mr Chipchase ever actually *said* he'd throw me out? Or had I just presumed it? Suddenly, I wasn't sure; I wasn't sure of anything. Especially not this great big change of heart.

'So what did convince you?' I asked.

Mr Chipchase folded his arms. 'That's my business, not yours.'

'I'll be walking the tightrope, will I? I'll be performing in the show?'

'Absolutely. You'll be front and centre stage.'

I could scarcely believe what I was hearing. When I could speak again, I said, 'And my other work in the circus? I'll do that too?'

'If you can manage it, at least for now.'

'Yes,' I said, very fast. 'I'll manage.' There'd be no reason then for him to change his mind.

'Excellent, excellent!'

It was too good to be true. I sat there in a daze until Gabriel nudged me. 'Say something, then,' he said.

I blinked. 'Um . . . well . . . I hardly know what to . . .'

Mr Chipchase interrupted me. 'You are happy with the arrangement, no?'

'Why, yes, sir!'

'That's settled.'

Not quite.

'One more thing, sir,' I said, bolder now. 'I'd like a proper costume. With sequins and ribbons.'

In the corner Kitty pulled a face. I didn't let it put me off.

'And I want my hair to look nice,' I kept on. 'No more plaiting it, no more hats. I want it all on show, like a proper performer.'

Mr Chipchase hesitated. He pressed his hand to his brow. For a moment I thought he was going to refuse.

'Very well,' he said, eventually.

Before I could thank him he changed course. 'Tomorrow we go to Littleton-on-Sea,' he said. 'A day's practice and then I want you both to perform, you and Gabriel.'

I wasn't quite keeping up. 'Me . . . and . . . ?'

I locked eyes with Gabriel. His smile slipped. There was pain in his look and I felt it too. It made me catch my breath.

Then he was smiling again. Mr Chipchase beamed broadly too. I checked there was no one standing behind me; there wasn't. That smile really was aimed at me.

But things still didn't quite add up. Excited as I was to have the chance to perform, finally, I was just a bit uneasy. Yet Mr Chipchase seemed happy; his smile reached up to the crinkly edges of his eyes. He'd once looked at Jasper like this. And Gabriel. Behind that smile was money.

'Excellent! We're agreed,' Mr Chipchase said,

shaking Gabriel's hand and then mine. 'Now I have *two* showstoppers. How many other circuses can boast of that?'

By 'other circuses' he meant Wellbeloved's; he always did.

*

The rest of the showground was in darkness. But I was far too excited for bed. Not wanting to wake Jasper, I tiptoed up our steps and slid inside before Pip had a chance to bark.

Jasper wasn't asleep. He was sitting by the stove, his leg resting on a stool. He looked drawn and pale. 'Where've you been?' he said.

'Just out.'

I wasn't quite able to meet his gaze. At my feet, Pip squirmed like I'd been gone *months*, and I felt awful. Just hours ago, I'd been set on leaving and not coming back. The sight of his doggy face made that unthinkable now.

'Folks were worried,' said Jasper. 'Ned was looking all over for you.'

He tried to sound cross but it just made me want to hug him. *Dear Jasper*. He did fret so. And I wouldn't blame him; if he knew the half of what I'd been up to tonight he'd never sleep again.

'Don't be grumpy,' I said. 'I've got the bestest news.'

He sighed. 'Go on then, what is it?'

I sat on my bunk. Pip jumped up beside me, determined not to let me out of his sight. I settled him on my lap and cleared my throat. This was a most serious announcement, after all.

'Mr Chipchase has offered me an exciting new role,' I said.

'Not more dog tricks?'

'No, silly,' I said, reaching for his hand. It felt thin, birdlike and very cold. 'This is something proper. A really big role.'

'Oh?'

'I'm so lucky I can hardly believe it. You see,' I swallowed. 'I'm going to be a showstopper.'

Jasper looked at me in disbelief. 'Really? But *how*?'

'You could be a bit more pleased,' I said.

He let go of my hand. Pulling his blanket tight around him, he stared into the fire. His jaw was clenched with worry. So I started talking. The words tumbled out of me in a breathless rush. 'I'll be performing with Gabriel Swift. He's so wonderful, honestly he is! And Mr Chipchase says that we're to perform together at Littleton-on-Sea, and then . . .'

Jasper was looking at me now. 'But Louie, sweetheart, you need to have a talent. You need to train. You can't just . . . *perform*.'

I took a deep breath. My secret had caught up with me, at last. Now I had some explaining to do. 'Jasper,' I said slowly. 'I haven't been exactly honest.'

'Perhaps you'd better start.'

I smoothed Pip's head for courage, for I suddenly felt a bit fluttery inside. 'The thing is, I can walk the tightrope. In fact, I can walk the tightrope very well.'

Jasper blinked. I kept going.

'I've been practising for quite some time. I keep a rope under the wagon, and once I've done the horses in the mornings I find a spot . . .' Seeing the shock on his face, I hesitated. 'Ned's watched me, and so has Gabriel Swift. And now Mr Chipchase knows about it and wants me to be part of the show.'

Jasper's fingers plucked at the blanket.

'Say something,' I said.

There were tears in his eyes. 'You're so brave, so grown up.'

'Not really,' I said. 'It's the tightrope. It makes me feel magic.'

Jasper smiled like he understood exactly what I

meant. If he was worried, he kept it hidden. And I was grateful for it.

'I didn't suppose you'd be happy selling tickets forever,' he said.

'This is my dream come true. On the tightrope it's like I can face anything.'

Jasper reached for my hand again, giving it a squeeze. 'Then it's time I stopped treating you like a little girl. There's something I need to share with you too. And it's not an easy thing.'

He looked so gaunt my thoughts took a gloomy turn. I felt nervous all over again. *Please tell me you're getting better, Jasper.*

'It's about your mother,' he said.

'Oh.' A moment of relief, then the dread came back. 'Her.'

'Louie, we have to talk about her.'

'Do we?'

'Yes, we do. She's your mother.'

I stared at him. 'But she ain't ever coming back. Mr Chipchase said she should've turned up by now and she ain't.'

'I want to show you something. It's high time you saw it,' Jasper said.

Leaning forward, he began searching under his bed.

He huffed and puffed but wouldn't let me help him. Finally, he sat up straight again with an old tea tin in his lap.

'I've been waiting for the right time to show you. Your mother left a letter,' he said.

A letter?

Jasper had never mentioned a letter before. My heart gave a thump.

'I don't want to see it,' I said.

Yet he'd already prised the lid off the tin. Inside I glimpsed a folded piece of paper. I began to sweat.

'She says she wants you to be happy,' he said, reaching into the tin. 'Perhaps that's all she's ever wanted.'

I stood up. 'I don't care to see it.'

'Louie, please.'

'My mother doesn't care a flying fig about my happiness.'

'That's not true!'

'Of course it's true. Why else would she have abandoned me? You can take her poxy letter and whatever other gubbins you've got in that tin, and keep them away from me!'

Jasper frowned. 'Perhaps you should calm down,' he said.

'Calm down?! Oh, and is that my dear mama's instruction too? Well, ain't it a big fat shame she's not here to tell me herself!'

I stomped outside, then marched up and down until my temper cooled. For once, it didn't take long. I was just about to go back inside when someone whispered, 'Louie!'

A figure in white stepped out of the darkness.

'Miss Lilly,' I said, inching back up the wagon steps. 'I must get to bed.'

'Please, look at this.'

She held out a single tarot card. I didn't want to see that, either. I kept my eyes on her.

'Not that death card again?'

'In Tarot, death doesn't mean dying. It means the end of something.' And she came right up to me, making it impossible to look away. 'But *this* is your final card.'

The picture was of a woman on a throne. The word EMPRESS was in big letters at the top of the card.

'As bad as the rest, is it?'

'No,' she said. 'It is the very best. It is the card of female power.'

The hair on my neck prickled. This didn't sound like *flimflam*, somehow.

'A strong woman is watching over you, Louie.'

'Who?'

'You know who she is.'

And though I hated to admit it, I was beginning to think maybe I did.

'You'll need her strength to help you,' Miss Lilly said. 'The cards foresee difficult times ahead.'

She left me then. And as I turned to go back inside, a shadow flitted across the grass. One moment it was there. Then it wasn't. But out of the tail of my eye, I knew I'd seen it, and my stomach tensed. For I swore that shadow had been wearing an impossibly tall top hat.

CHAPTER 15

Gabriel and me waited backstage. Any moment it'd be our turn for real. We'd arrived at Littleton-on-Sea yesterday, and our stand between the promenade and the sand dunes was the finest I'd ever seen.

'You ready?' I asked Gabriel, for I certainly was. Though two people on the rope was harder than I'd realised, we'd glowed off each other like candles in a mirror. I still felt the flame of it now.

Gabriel shuffled his feet. 'Ready as ninepence.'

He didn't look it. An ugly red mark stood out on his throat.

'What happened to your neck?' I said.

His hand flew up to hide it. 'What? Oh, I tied my scarf too tight.'

Really? But he never wore a scarf.

As I went to say so, the curtains drew back. Gabriel took my hand. His fingers felt icy cold. I wondered if he was nervous. Surely not. Not *the* Gabriel Swift from Wellbeloved's Circus. The light caught his tunic, making it sparkle blue. Mine was the same, only with short flouncing skirts. I'd been up half the night working on them both. And now, at last, my hair fell loose down my back. Every part of me felt like a showstopper.

Inside the ring, Mighty Ned announced us. 'Ladies and gentlemen, a brand new act . . .' His voice rose and dipped. My heart did the same. The crowd started clapping. The drums beat faster, trumpets blared, and then came the crash of cymbals: our cue.

As I stepped forward, something yanked me back. Gabriel hadn't moved. He was still holding my hand.

'I can't do it, Louie,' he said.

He was joking. *Wasn't he?* I tried tugging him but he wouldn't shift. The cymbals crashed a second time. Gabriel's face was tight with fear. I started to panic myself. If we didn't get out in that ring THIS MINUTE my chance as a showstopper would be over before it had even started.

'Come on, you *can* do it,' I said.

Gabriel shook his head. 'I can't.'

The cymbals crashed a third time.

'Gabriel?' I said, low and firm. 'It worked in rehearsal. And it'll work in the ring.'

He shut his eyes and shuddered.

'So let's get out there and do our show.'

I tugged him again. He stumbled a step or two then gave in. Somehow I got him into the ring. Mighty Ned shot me a '*Where were you?*' look, but no one in the crowd had noticed. I just prayed Gabriel wouldn't seize up again.

The lights went down. One single spot of brightness shone in the middle of the ring. Gabriel and me, in our matching costumes, stood under it.

Mighty Ned spread his arms out to the spectators. 'I give you . . .' the drums rolled, 'for the first time . . . Miss Louie Lightfoot . . . and the Great Fun Ambler . . .'

We bowed at the applause. Gabriel seemed to settle, waving his free arm and looking more the showman. Then the light split into two smaller spots. One fell on Gabriel, one on me. He let go of my hand. Stepping properly apart, I shook back my hair and bowed graciously to each corner of the tent. A fluttering grew in my chest. I felt truly alive.

From his sickbed, Jasper had given me some advice. 'Find a face in the crowd,' he'd said. 'Make your performance just for them.'

So I scanned the front row. It was faces galore: pretty, young misses, smart, whiskered gents, children in sailor suits. Yet none of these faces stood out.

Then I saw Mr Chipchase. Odd for him to sit at the front with the towners. Usually he watched backstage. Tonight he sat bolt upright in his seat. He was even wearing his best tartan waistcoat. Next to him was a dark, whiskered man whose hands rested on the top of a walking cane. On his head he wore a very tall hat.

My heart skipped a beat. I knew that hat all right. It was *him*, the flashy cove from Blondin's show. The man who'd blocked my view, then trailed me through town.

What the heck was he doing here?

I'd no idea. But like it or not, I'd found my face. I'd show him he didn't scare me tonight.

The music struck up again. The drums beat faster and the lights began to move around the ring. We crossed to our rope ladders at either end of the tightrope. My blood quickened. Hundreds of eyes were on me; I felt them like heat on my back. The lights followed us up our ladders. Every fourth rung, I paused to wave and smile. The flames in me kept flickering till I was all lit up inside.

At the top I stepped out onto the platform, feeling the wood through the soles of my slippers. Then I closed my eyes. Straightened my back. Took a long draught of air.

Seventy feet below, Mighty Ned's voice sang on. I pictured the scene: towners sat on the edge of their seats, Mr Chipchase stroking his whiskers. All of them watching, waiting – but one face more than any other: the tall-hatted man gripping his cane. With a jolt, I remembered how he'd ranted at Blondin with a sneering, jealous spite. And it didn't help to think of it now.

Focus, Louie.

Opening my eyes, I looked up ahead. On the platform opposite, Gabriel was ready. A little nod and he stepped out onto the rope. I counted to five, then walked out from my side.

All that mattered now was the rope.

Feeling with my foot, I placed it toe to heel on the line. My knees flexed. Slowly, lightly, I slid my front foot forward. The line shivered. Every twitch of it went through my feet and up into my legs. Every step Gabriel took did the same.

Below us, Mighty Ned told our story. Snatches of words drifted upwards.

'Out walking . . . saw each other . . . love at first sight . . .'

We met in the middle. The rope trembled, doubly so for having two people on it. I waited for it to go quiet. This was the part where we were meant to stare lovingly at each other. I reached out to touch Gabriel's cheek. But he wasn't even looking my way; he was staring down at the crowd.

The next steps were tricky.

'Times were hard. They couldn't be together . . .' Mighty Ned went on.

The plan was to walk round each other, Gabriel going first. He didn't move. 'Gabriel?'

No answer. He was still looking downwards.

'Slide your foot forward,' I hissed. 'And look at me.'

The rope began to sway. I bent my knees to go with it. Gabriel didn't move. His eyes had that glazed look that made me suddenly fearful. If he didn't flex with the rope sway he'd fall.

Desperate now, I tried another tack. 'Your platform's just behind you. Five steps and you'll be there.'

Really, it was more like ten. But it worked. Gabriel blinked, took a big breath and did exactly as I said. Once on solid wood he slumped to his knees, looking sick as a dog.

Bit by bit, the rope grew still again.

Focus now, Louie.

My head cleared. First, I went backwards. It kept with the story of us parting company. But then I was lost. We were meant to go 'calling' on each other, take walks with parasols, read books, skip happily along. Right now there was more chance of snow in July.

Below in the ring Mighty Ned looked up as if to say '*What now?*' I signalled him to keep talking. He knew the routine as well as I did. We could do it between us. A nod of the head told me he understood. I could've cried with relief.

Ned's banter came easy. 'Miss Louie couldn't forget how her love had left her. She kept walking in the vain hope of meeting him once more . . .'

The rest was down to me.

Laid out on the platform were my props. I grabbed the parasol. Holding it high above my head, I walked out onto the rope. The crowd clapped. Three steps along, I opened the parasol and twirled it. I walked backwards, placing one foot, then the other, all the way to Gabriel's platform.

'Just stay there. Don't move,' I said. If I was going to do this right, far better that I do it by myself. Gabriel nodded his agreement.

More twirls of the parasol. I walked backwards and

forwards till I'd reached my side again. The audience cheered.

The next props were paper and pen.

'There was no sign of him . . .' Mighty Ned sang out. 'So Miss Louie decided to write to her love . . .'

Out in the middle I squatted down. One leg trailed beneath me for balance. Spreading the paper over my knee, I pretended to write. Every now and then I paused, chewed the pen, gazed off into the distance. Not once did I look at Gabriel, or down at the tall-hatted man. I didn't need to.

Something special was starting to happen. I felt it grow. The big top was hushed. Four hundred people stared up at me. Four hundred hearts beating as fast as mine. The air prickled with it.

Keep focused, Louie.

I pretended to grow tired, then tucked the paper in my skirts and lay back on the rope. It cut into my head, my neck, the base of my spine.

'Each night, she dreamed of him . . .' said Mighty Ned.

The crowd gasped. The slightest tip and I'd fall. But the rope kept steady. I breathed slow. Counted to ten. Another ten. Then I got to my feet and did a curtsey. The crowd cheered.

Now for the finale.

'Just when she'd given up hope,' said Mighty Ned, 'a letter arrived. A letter telling her that one day he'd be back to claim her.'

In the middle of the rope I opened the pretend letter, held it to my heart, and acted out a swoon. The crowd cried out 'No!' thinking me about to fall. Then they laughed in relief as I let go of the letter and it fluttered to the ground.

Mighty Ned bantered on. 'Thank you ladies and gentlemen ... do come tomorrow to see more of ... the wonderful ... the *sensational* ... Miss ... Louie ... Lightfoot!'

A crash of cymbals and the music started up. But I wasn't done yet. A proper finale always had the crowd gasping, sweating, barely believing their eyes. And down in that ring was one particular face. I wanted him to see my courage.

The trick was difficult. Of course Blondin had done it, and I'd tried it a few times myself in private. It had always worked. Now was different. With four hundred people watching, the thrill was huge.

I stood very still. Felt the rope. *Thought* the rope. Imagined it as part of me, a living, twitching thing. The music stopped. Then came the thickest silence, like a great big breath held in. Swinging my arms, I flipped over backwards.

My feet landed square on the rope. It sagged, then bounced. I bent my knees. My arms flew out. The rope steadied. I waited just a beat before somersaulting forwards.

A whoosh of air. Faces, sawdust, all was a blur. One foot found the rope. The other floundered in thin air. I lurched sideways. Then, somehow, I was upright again.

The crowd made a noise fit to lift the roof. It was the sweetest sound I'd ever heard. Every single person was on their feet. You'd have thought Blondin himself was here. But he wasn't.

This was all for me.

CHAPTER 16

Backstage was all kisses and smiles. How different it felt. Just days ago I'd been as wretched as can be. Now I was dizzy with happiness.

As the next act got started, I finally collared Ned.

'I owe you a million thank-yous,' I beamed.

He didn't smile back. 'The show must go on, Louie, even if some people aren't up to it.'

He looked at my hand, still clamped around Gabriel's, then turned on his heel and walked off. It left me feeling rather sore. There was no pleasing Ned Bailey these days.

Turning to Gabriel, I asked, 'What happened out there?'

He looked deathly white. This wasn't a case of eating bad cockles from the seafront. Something was very wrong.

'It's a long story, I'm afraid.' He untangled his fingers from mine.

'Are you going to tell me about it?'

He frowned. 'Mr Wellbeloved has caught up with me.'

'Caught up? What, to ask after your health?'

'Hardly!' Gabriel spluttered. 'What I mean is, he's here in Littleton to claim me back.'

This didn't make sense.

'For what?' No offence to Gabriel, but in this state he wasn't much use on the tightrope.

'To perform.' He saw the look on my face. 'Oh, don't worry, he'll make me do it, no matter what.'

'That ain't right, not if you don't want to. You must tell him, Gabriel. It ain't fair!'

Gabriel shrugged. He looked hopeless. It made me want to help him, but I didn't know how.

'So how did he find you?' Now I was frowning too. 'You said he'd let you go. And we gave you a new name just to be sure.'

'He followed me. Followed us. Said he questioned people who might've seen me, that sort of thing.'

My head started spinning.

Questions, eh? And to follow a travelling circus, you'd need . . .

I went awful cold.

. . . a carriage.

Oh heck. Could Ned's fancy gent and Mr Wellbeloved be the same person? *Oh hecking HECK!*

Which brought me back to Ned. I felt suddenly sick. This was his doing, wasn't it? What *was* he thinking? He should've kept his gob shut that day in the village. And he NEVER should've told Mr Chipchase. Even if it had helped me, which I very much doubted, it certainly hadn't helped Gabriel. But then perhaps that was his plan.

I'd plenty to say to Ned Bailey, and none of it would be polite. Gabriel, meantime, was edging towards the exit.

'I'm sorry Louie, but I really must . . .'

He stopped dead. The other performers parted like a sea. What colour he had left now drained from Gabriel's face. Mr Chipchase came towards us. At his side was the tall-hatted man. I put on my best smile, but Mr Chipchase elbowed past me and went straight to Gabriel.

'Look who's come all this way to watch you tonight,' Mr Chipchase said with a strained smile.

I waited for him to praise me. He didn't.

'Gabriel's performances have been exceptional,' he said to the tall-hatted man.

Really? I pulled a face. *Did Mr Chipchase think this*

man was blind? But when I stepped forward, so he couldn't keep ignoring me, he blocked my way. I grew more frustrated.

'I can only apologise. I'd no idea he'd run away from you, Mr Wellbeloved,' said Mr Chipchase.

It was true then. This man in the too-tall hat was Mr Wellbeloved. THE Mr Wellbeloved.

I ducked under Mr Chipchase's arm for a better look. So this was Ned's gent who'd asked questions. He was also the man I'd run away from in Sharpfield. Come to think of it, perhaps Gabriel had too; he'd certainly scarpered from the show pretty quick. He really was Mr Wellbeloved, whose name hung over our circus like smoke.

Yet why pretend that Gabriel had been such a success? Why all the big talk for him, who'd spent the show shivering on his platform, and none for me?

'Apology accepted,' Mr Wellbeloved said, touching the brim of his hat.

I trembled in excitement and a little bit of fear. For in the world of the circus, Mr Wellbeloved was royalty. Love him or loathe him, he had money and power, which oozed out of him like sweat.

To think how I'd given him lip when he'd blocked my view of Blondin! And how rudely I'd run off down an alley when he'd shown his concern. God knows what might've happened if I'd gone with him that night. I might even be *his* showstopper now. I must have sunk into a daydream of giddy thoughts, for it was then that Mr Wellbeloved's attention fell on me.

'And the girl?' he said, pointing at me with his cane. 'Her performance was most intriguing.'

It was a joy to hear praise at last.

Dodging around Mr Chipchase, I gave a little bow, and dearly hoped my talents had wiped clean any memory of Sharpfield. If Mr Wellbeloved did recognise me, he didn't show it. His face was a mask. It was Mr Chipchase who seemed agitated.

'It was her first performance,' he said. 'Beginner's luck probably. Anyway, back to Gabriel . . .'

I cut in. 'Nice to meet you, Mr Wellbeloved. I'm glad you liked the show.'

He nodded. The corners of his mouth twitched. Then his attention moved to Gabriel.

'Good evening, Master Swift,' he said.

'Good evening,' said Gabriel.

It all seemed very polite. We might've been taking tea together, though I still felt confused.

'Now listen,' Mr Chipchase said. 'Mr Wellbeloved

has an offer to make. A very attractive offer, as it stands.'

Aha, the money part, I thought. Ned had mentioned a reward. Yet why was Mr Chipchase calling it an 'offer'? It was still money for 'claiming' Gabriel Swift, who clearly didn't want to go anywhere.

'I came here tonight for Mr Swift,' Mr Wellbeloved explained, 'who, despite what he might have told you, is still under my employ.'

Gabriel flinched and took a step backwards.

'Instead, I am greeted by this surprising performance. It has great potential, and I'm very interested in taking it to a bigger venue.'

My ears perked up.

'But to be clear,' he continued, 'the offer is for one special performer.'

One of us? Which one? I was more confused than ever. Mr Chipchase took out a handkerchief and wiped his brow. I glanced at Gabriel. He was still eyeing the door, his only way out.

'That offer is to come to America, where truly great things will await you.' Mr Wellbeloved looked directly at me. 'In return, I will expect you to be ready for the challenge.'

America!

'Oh lordy,' I said. 'That . . . would be . . . quite something!'

America! It was a faraway dream of a place. Blondin had gone there a nobody and come back a truly famous name. I couldn't imagine anything finer. Yet I seemed to be the only person thinking it. Mr Chipchase kept wiping his face and Gabriel looked horribly grey.

For a beat, my eyes met Mr Wellbeloved's. He gave a tiny nod of the head. I hardly dared breathe.

Would he choose me?

Gabriel Swift had the reputation, the looks, the experience. Yet he lacked the sensation part, the *whiff of death*. And tonight he'd gone to pieces. I didn't suppose for one moment he'd want to go to America now. It pained me to see him so troubled. But if Mr Wellbeloved did choose me, it would let Gabriel off the hook. He'd never have to walk a tightrope again.

Simple.

'Louie has little experience,' said Mr Chipchase, bringing me round with a jolt. 'And she is still very young for such a challenge.'

Mr Wellbeloved narrowed his eyes. 'Louie, eh? Short for . . . ?'

'Louisa, sir,' I said, before Mr Chipchase could answer.

'I see.'

Mr Wellbeloved pinched the bridge of his nose, like a person with a headache, and gave a great sigh.

'Are you sick, sir?' I said, going to help him.

Mr Chipchase's arm shot out and yanked me back, nearly knocking me off my feet.

'Quite well,' said Mr Wellbeloved. 'I'd advise you both to get a good night's rest. One of you will be leaving with me on the first train for Liverpool tomorrow. I shall make my decision in the morning.'

And with a touch of his hat brim, he was gone.

*

Gabriel slunk off without a word. I did the same, having nothing left to say to Mr Chipchase, who'd been so set on putting me down. I ducked out the back door – and straight into a woman.

'Goodness, they don't teach you manners here, do they?' she cried.

In her buttoned-up black coat she was clearly a do-gooder. Before I had a chance to reply, the canvas flapped open and light spilled over us.

'What ho? No problems here are there?' Mr Chipchase said. He seemed jumpy as anything. Then he saw the do-gooder and sighed. 'Oh, it's only *your* kind again. Here, take this,' he said, giving her a handful of coins.

The woman stared at them. I did too, for just days ago he'd claimed we were desperately poor.

'I won't be bribed,' said the woman.

'For your charity', he said. 'Please, take it. With my blessing.'

Blessing? Since when had he wished do-gooders well?

After plenty of fuss, the woman took the money. 'It doesn't mean I won't report you. That boy on the tightrope was terrified,' she said, then fixed on me, taking in my short skirts and loose hair. 'And you, young lady, look quite improper. You should be at school.'

I toed the grass uneasily, yet Mr Chipchase seemed remarkably unconcerned. 'It'll blow over once Gabriel's in America,' he said, after the woman had gone. 'There are worse things to concern ourselves with than do-gooders.'

'Mr Wellbeloved ain't decided yet,' I reminded him. 'He might choose me.'

'Forget it. You'll be staying here. You work for Chipchase's.'

I folded my arms. 'As a showstopper though, right?'

He didn't answer me for a long time, and I was sure he'd forgotten I was here.

'Well?' I said.

He rubbed his face and sighed. 'I don't know, Louie.'

I kicked at the ground. If he thought I'd go back to being invisible again, he was wrong.

'But Mr Wellbeloved saw my talents. *He* noticed me. He had a glint in his eye just from looking at me,' I said.

'Did he now?'

'He did. And that's a good thing, ain't it?'

By the look on Mr Chipchase's face it clearly wasn't. 'How can I put it?' he said, stroking his whiskers. 'Mr Wellbeloved is a gentleman of the shade.'

I scowled. 'Meaning?'

'He's not just rich and successful. He has a dark side too, though you obviously hadn't noticed.'

The way he'd looked at Blondin's daughter flashed into my mind. I pushed the memory aside.

'I knew it would cause trouble, letting you have your way,' said Mr Chipchase. 'We should've stuck to the dog tricks. It would've saved us a lot of bother.'

I stared at him, open-mouthed. Had he gone completely insane? 'The crowd LOVED me, sir. Didn't you see it?' I clasped my hands to my chest. 'Didn't you feel it?'

He gave another great sigh. 'You're a beginner at this game, Louie. Your time will come.'

'I've been practising for years!' I cried. 'And I'm tired of being held back all the time!'

'I mean it for the best.'

'But you put me in a clown suit and make me hide my hair. And then you push me to one side when Mr Wellbeloved turns up. It's like you're ashamed of me!' I blinked back angry tears. 'It ain't fair!'

Mr Chipchase's face went very red. I knew I'd gone too far. But whatever he thought, I *had* caught Mr Wellbeloved's eye. It didn't matter to him which one of us went to America; he'd get his cut either way.

Yet as I made to go, Mr Chipchase patted my shoulder quite gently. 'You did well tonight, Louie,' he said. 'Your mother would be proud.'

'Shame she couldn't make it,' I said sarcastically. 'What kept her?'

He looked at me gravely. 'I've often wondered that myself.'

CHAPTER 17

The second I got into our wagon Pip was upon me. Jasper got up from his seat too and hobbled the few steps between us.

'I heard them cheering you, Louie. You must've put on a great show,' he said.

I couldn't help but smile. 'Don't overdo it. Come on, sit down.'

'You sound just like me,' he laughed, and holding my hand planted three kisses on the palm.

It was good to be home.

'Now, tell me everything,' Jasper said, once I'd settled him back in his chair. 'How did it feel? What were the best bits? Did it all go to plan?'

For the first time in ages, he looked bright-eyed and pink-cheeked. As I sat at his feet, Pip curled up at mine. I started from the beginning, and saved the best part till last.

'You'll not believe it, but Mr Wellbeloved was in

the crowd. *The* Mr Wellbeloved!'

'Crikey! Is that so?'

I nodded eagerly. 'He was mightily impressed. He wants to take one of us to America!'

Jasper whistled. 'America, eh? Phew!'

He fell quiet.

I twisted round to face him. 'What do you make of that, then?'

'I don't know,' he said.

'If he does choose me, I won't go. Not if you don't want me to.'

'I can't keep you here, Louie, and it's not fair to try. My days as a performer are over, but yours are just beginning.'

'But if you're still sick . . .'

Jasper sat up straight in his chair, as if to make a point. 'Do you think he'll choose you?' he asked.

'Maybe. But if I do go, I'll be back soon.'

And I meant it. These were my people here. My very bones.

For a while we sat quietly. Yet my head was busy with all sorts of thinking, including Miss Lilly and her cards. The first one she'd shown me was of a man striding over a cliff edge. The fool going into the unknown. And the last one was of a strong woman, the empress, who'd watch over me. If I believed in that flimflam.

I took a deep breath. 'I'd like to read my mam's letter,' I said.

Behind me, I sensed Jasper go very still. 'Are you sure?'

'I am.'

*

There wasn't much inside the old tea tin. Just a folded-up piece of paper and a little scrap of cloth.

I read the letter first.

Friday 12 November 1865

Kindest Sir,
You find here my little baby girl. Please accept her. Hard though it is for me to part with her, I know you will love her dear.
My life has taken a very sorry turn. Desperate as I am, I have no choice now but to go far, far away. To stay would be to risk my own life, to take her with me would risk that of my dearest girl.

Your circus is a fine example of its kind. I see magic here and people who know what it is to care for one another. Even your horses seem happy. I pray you have goodwill enough to share, for I am in terrible trouble and so in need of your help.

My little girl's name is Louisa. I call her Louie. Keep her safe for me. Bring her up to be good. Always let her follow her heart. Give her your own fine surname if you will. Someday, I will claim her back again.

Until that day, love her well.

Yours

M.S.

When I could bear to, I read it again. And again, more slowly this time. The words didn't seem to sink in.

Eventually, Jasper touched my shoulder. 'It's not what you'd thought, is it?' he said.

'No.'

It was as if a bird was flying about inside my chest. I'd expected to find coldness in that letter, or some feeble excuse. Yet she'd called me her little baby girl, and said 'dear' and 'love'. It was like reading big long words I didn't quite understand.

'You should have told me before,' I said.

'I did try.'

I suppose Mr Chipchase had tried too, and I'd not listened to him.

'Well, you should've made me hear it. All this time, I've hated her, and . . .' I trailed off. I didn't know who to be angry with now. Truth was, I didn't even *feel* angry. In a daze, I picked up the scrap of cloth. Held up to the lamplight, it didn't look so dull. It was a rich red taffeta. Flattened out, it was shaped like a heart.

'That night I found you, it was tucked inside your blankets,' Jasper said.

I smoothed it over my knee, and kept stroking it just to see its shape. 'Can I keep it?'

'I'm sure she meant it for you.'

A lump grew in my throat. She seemed to love me. My own mother had actually loved me. I felt completely floored, and began to cry in earnest. Jasper rubbed my back until I stopped, then he handed me a handkerchief to wipe my face.

I took a big breath. The tears made my chest ache. 'Do you know any more about her?'

Jasper shook his head. 'I'd only just joined the circus myself. I didn't know much about anything, only the trapeze.'

'That night, did you even *see* her?'

Again, a shake of the head. 'It was a foggy winter's night. The show had just ended. When I got back to the wagon I found a basket on the steps. You were inside.'

'But you didn't even know her. Why did she choose your wagon?'

'I don't know. The fog was very thick. Perhaps it was just the first one she came to.'

Perhaps.

I glanced down at the letter, tracing her curly writing with my finger. She'd touched this paper once. *My own mother.*

My finger stopped. 'Do you know why she was in trouble?'

'I've no idea. A young woman, down on her luck, with a baby. It's not as unusual as you'd think, sadly.'

'Did she ever work here?'

'I'm sorry, I don't know, Louie. To this day I've never been entirely sure why Mr Chipchase agreed to take you in.'

Tolerate me, more like. At least that's how it was

up until two days ago, when he'd finally given me a chance to show my talent. What a sudden change of heart he'd had. Though after tonight he might well change it back again.

'Perhaps Mr Chipchase was flattered. She's said very nice things about his circus. Have you asked him?' I said.

Jasper pressed his fingers to his brow. 'He wouldn't talk about it. He clammed up, just like you do, Louie, when something's too much. But he's always assumed she'd come back for you.'

'So why hasn't she?'

He squeezed my shoulder.

'Do you think she's still alive?' I said.

'She might be. We don't know.'

Miss Lilly's cards had shown a strong woman watching over me. She had to be still out there somewhere.

'I'd know if she was dead,' I said. 'I'm certain she's not.'

Jasper watched me closely. 'The world's a very big place, Louie. I doubt you'd ever find her.'

'I can dream.'

Yet he knew me. And I knew myself: once I'd seized a thing, I wouldn't let it go. In my mind, I pictured

Mam thinking me lost without trace.

But perhaps *I* might find *her*.

I'd certainly stand more chance of it travelling the world than I would staying here with Chipchase's.

'Don't get ahead of yourself,' Jasper warned.

He meant it for the best, I knew. Yet for some reason my mam hadn't come back for me. I'd always assumed it was because she didn't care. But maybe that wasn't it at all. Maybe something was keeping her, stopping her from coming back. Mr Chipchase seemed to think so.

I was beginning to wonder it too.

*

When I woke it was barely daybreak. My head started churning right away.

My mam loved me. My mam loves me.

It still hadn't sunk in. I'd not get back to sleep now either.

The horses were surprised to get their oats and hay quite so early. Once I'd finished feeding them, I took Pip for a walk along the beach. The sky was just pinking up in the east. Aside from the gulls, we were the only creatures out here. The sea, flat as quicksilver, lapped at my bare toes. With a shiver, I gazed at the horizon and thought of all that lay beyond.

After a goodly while, I turned for home and saw a flattened square of grass among the dunes. It was the size of a small tent. Or rather, where a small tent had been. Pip ran over to it and began sniffing madly. My stomach flipped over. I started to run. The closer I got, the more obvious it was. No tent meant no Gabriel.

He'd gone.

The sadness of it hit me and I filled up with tears. Yet despite the shock, it did make sense. No true performer could bear any more shows like last night. When things went that wrong, it was time to quit. At least he might be happier.

Taking a deep breath, I dried my face on my sleeve. So, what now of Mr Wellbeloved's choice?

Yesterday, there'd been two of us to choose from; today there was only one. He'd have to choose me; there was no one else. I felt a sudden panic. Then thrilling excitement. I didn't hear the footsteps behind me. Ned's voice made me catch my breath.

'Gabriel went just before sunrise,' he said.

I looked round, thinking he'd be pleased, but he still seemed sour. It felt a long time ago now since we'd shared a proper laugh. I was sorry for it.

'Did he say where he was heading?' I asked.

'Don't you know?'

'Know what?'

'He went with Mr Wellbeloved.'

I didn't quite follow. 'Mr Wellbeloved? Where?'

'You *don't* know, do you?'

For a moment I thought he was trying to spare my feelings. Then I saw the glee in his eyes, and the dread landed *doof* in my stomach.

'Mr Wellbeloved came for him this morning. They caught the Liverpool train about an hour ago. They're going to America.'

I stared at him blankly. So they'd gone together. Without me.

'I'd go back to bed if I was you,' said Ned.

Except he wasn't me. Now that America was in my brain there was no changing it. I wasn't about to go back to being a nobody. I wanted crowds. Fame. The *whiff of death*, even. Poor Gabriel didn't. It terrified him, and I wondered if maybe he'd gone against his will. Then there was Mam. I couldn't forget her, not now I'd read her letter.

Ned started to walk away.

'You were right about the fancy gent,' I called out.

He stopped.

'Turns out he was Mr Wellbeloved looking for Gabriel. Thanks to you, he found him.'

Ned's mouth was set in a grim line. 'I'm glad of it too.'

'But you're not right about everything,' I said, 'so don't think you are.'

For one thing, I wasn't going back to bed.

✳ INTERVAL ✳

CHAPTER 18

The next train for Liverpool left at just after eight. Catching it was the easy part. A quick dip under the arm of a man carrying parcels and I managed to sneak into one of the third-class carriages. At first, the train stopped plenty. Each time the conductor asked for 'Tickets, please', I ducked down to tie my bootlace. Then the proper countryside began and the stops got fewer. As I sat quietly the doubts began.

No one had seen me leave the showground. I'd put on my plainest frock and wrapped some cheese and bread in a cloth for the journey. Jasper was fast asleep, so I left a note beside his teacup. Then I kissed his palm three times; *that* had been tough enough, but dear Pip followed me right to the door. Just the thought of him made my throat go thick.

Fields sped past the window in a blur of green and brown. My heart was sinking now. Mr Wellbeloved didn't want me; I was fooling myself. He'd chosen

Gabriel Swift, who had experience and proper training. I should go home. Forget about it. Go back to selling tickets and sewing sequins. Life would be easier if I did.

Easier maybe. But not happier. Last night my eyes had been truly opened. The crowds loved me, and so did my own mam. I was still reeling from the shock of it. To turn away now would be madness, like cutting myself in half and never being whole again.

And there was Gabriel. It just didn't seem right that he'd agreed to go with Mr Wellbeloved. Not when last night he'd been so scared. Or maybe Mr Wellbeloved really had chosen Gabriel. If so, then he'd made a mighty mistake. I needed to tell him and offer myself instead. He'd realise and be glad. Then Gabriel would be free, and I'd go to America in his place.

The train slowed ready for the next stop. The chugging wheels seemed to echo my thoughts: *Stay or go? Stay or go?* Stuffed down my shift was my mam's red taffeta heart. I'd put my faith in it. If a strong woman really was watching over me, I'd be all right.

*

Five long hours after leaving Littleton, I finally reached Liverpool docks. It was a grim place. Red brick buildings blocked out the sun, making the water look too black and the quayside feel too small. There were two types of passenger, or so it seemed: those carrying bundles on their backs, and those whose bags were carried for them. The place was heaving. How I'd ever find Mr Wellbeloved I'd no idea.

Three ships sat alongside the dock. The biggest had a great steam funnel and two masts. This, I guessed, was the ship going to America. Men ran to and fro, carrying trunks and boxes and mattresses on board. Stood near the gangplank was another man handing out cards saying 'Visitor Pass'.

I went up to him. 'What ship is this please, mister?'

He didn't look up from his notes. 'The SS *Marathon*. Bound for New York.'

'Any others going to America today?'

'Just this one.'

So it had to be the right ship.

'Can you tell me who's on it?'

He looked up. His eyes slid over my frock. I wasn't one of the smart passengers and he knew it.

'I'd like to say goodbye to a Mr Gideon Wellbeloved,' I said, sniffing pretend tears.

'Mr Wellbeloved?' The man seemed suddenly impressed and scanned his list. 'Yes, of course. Upper deck, cabin 12A.'

And just like that he gave me a visitor pass.

Once on board, I followed the signs, heading straight for cabin 12A. At first, the passageways were narrow and stank of oil. Countless times I flattened myself against the wall as more boxes and crates and goodness knows what went past. As I reached the upper deck the passageways widened. There was carpet underfoot, wood panels on the walls, and paintings and carvings making the ship look like a townhouse. I gazed about me in awe.

Little knots of people started to appear. And my word, these were rich-looking folks, especially the women, with their narrow skirts all bumped out at the back and hair curled at their necks.

'May I assist you?' asked a man wearing a badge that said 'Steward'. When I showed him my visitor pass, he insisted on escorting me right to the cabin itself.

'Cabin 12A,' he said, as if I couldn't read the brass sign on the door. He knocked once then pushed the door open.

The cabin was empty.

The steward looked at his watch. 'You've ten

minutes. The ship sails at half past one.'

Someone called him then, so he left me. My fingers went to the front of my shift. Mam's taffeta heart was still there. It felt cool to the touch. *Think sharp, Louie.* Ten minutes wasn't long. Once I'd found Mr Wellbeloved, I still had to convince him to take me instead of Gabriel.

The cabin floor was heaped with luggage labelled 'Wellbeloved'. In among it, I recognised Gabriel's kitbag. Which meant this was definitely their cabin. And they must be here on board. But where?

Back out in the passage, another sign said 'Dining Saloon' and it had a picture of a finger pointing ahead. I followed the hum of many voices, praying Mr Wellbeloved's was one of them.

The dining saloon was another grand affair, with carved pillars and vases full of flowers. White-clothed tables were set for lunch, yet no one was sat down. Women, men, children with their nannies, all stood around chatting. More men in waistcoats moved among them with trays of champagne. There were plenty of top hats; though none were especially tall. By now I was hot and very bothered. Where the devil was Mr Wellbeloved?

In a far corner a boy had his back to me. There

was something familiar about the way he ran a hand through his hair. My heart leaped: *Gabriel!*

Rushing over, I almost collided with a steward.

'Steady miss!' he cried, his drinks tray lurching.

I didn't stop, elbowing past all the satins and silks until the boy was right before me.

Already grinning, I tugged his sleeve. 'Gabriel?'

The boy turned round.

He wasn't Gabriel. Not even slightly. I went very red.

'Sorry,' I muttered. 'You ain't who I thought.'

The boy sniffed. 'Clearly,' he said, and turned his back.

By now, other people were staring too, all with the same snooty look on their faces. I grew hotter and crosser. And to cap it all, the steward was back with his tray of glasses.

'May I see your pass?' he said.

I went to give it to him. A minute ago it'd been in my hand. Now the blasted thing wasn't here.

'Just hang on.' I searched my pockets.

No sign of it.

'I had it, I swear I did,' I said in growing panic.

The steward was already signalling with his eyes to another man by the door. 'The fun's over, miss. Time to get off the ship,' he said.

Wildly, I looked around for Mr Wellbeloved. I had to find him, fast.

The steward put his drinks tray down. His mate by the door was now halfway across the room. My heart started racing. Two of them. One of me. There was nothing else for it.

I ran.

Once through the doors, I turned right. Anywhere just to keep moving. More of those finger signs pointed the way to the deck. I ran faster, my boots thudding hard on the carpet. The passage ended in two flights of steps. One was a proper staircase. The other was a narrow set of steps. I took these. Only one steward was behind me now. I needed to shake him off my tail. I took the steps two at a time. At the top was a little door. The handle was stiff and it took me a moment to force it open. Once I was through, I slammed the door behind me.

The deck was packed with people. Some leaned over the railings, calling goodbyes towards the quay. Others stood in huddles, singing songs or saying prayers. My hopes sank. No sign of a tall top hat here either.

Somewhere on deck a bell started ringing.

'Last call for visitor passes,' came the cry.

Abruptly, the bell stopped ringing. As if on cue, people began sobbing. All around me white hankies waved at the quayside, where more hankies waved back. Time was running out. If I didn't find Mr Wellbeloved very fast, I'd be back on dry land with nothing.

The steward had almost caught up now, but he still hadn't spotted me in the crowd. I did the first thing I could think of. Just like everyone else, I waved at the quay. He did too, or rather gestured with his arms. A few hearty shouts and the gangplank was raised. Smoke belched from the ship's funnel. The deck seemed to shudder. At first, I thought my eyes were playing tricks. Then, bit by bit, the quay slipped away. The ship was moving and I was stuck on board. And I still hadn't found Mr Wellbeloved.

Yet come what may, we were sailing. Next stop America.

CHAPTER 19

One thing I learned pretty quick on board ship: steerage class was for poor people. First class was for rich folks. Each had their own bit of deck to roam about on. Steerage's was right next to the engines, which was where I found myself now. It was separated from first class by gates; tall, locked gates. So I was on one side. And Mr Wellbeloved and Gabriel were on the other. It wasn't exactly a help.

One gate stood near the coal heap. The other, on the opposite side of the ship, was next to the mast. Stewards passed through them quite often. They made a show of all the locking and unlocking, which I supposed was meant to impress the rich passengers. And that afternoon there were plenty up on deck, pointing and crying things like 'It's Mount Snowdon!' or 'I swear that town's Fishguard!', though to me it just looked like land. Truth was, I was too twitchy for sightseeing. I was worried for my own skin, and for Gabriel's too. The sooner I found him the better.

Every hour, I'd give each gate a shake. I double-checked the bolts and chains too. But the gates were locked. Always locked. And twelve feet high with spikes on top, the bars slippery from the sea air. I'd never get over one, or even through one.

By nine o'clock it was dark, and most people had retired. I found a quiet spot by the coal heap, but it wasn't in the slightest bit comfy. There was no Pip curled up next to me either. It made me long for home so much it hurt.

Touching Mam's red heart, I breathed out long and slow. It calmed my thoughts. Then I noticed cooking smells wafting up through the hatches, and grew properly starving. I'd eaten the last of my bread and cheese hours ago. All I could think of now was pies and gravy, or a nice leg of chicken with the skin all crisp.

A voice in the dark made me start.

'You still up here?'

A lamp shone over me. I scrambled to my feet. 'I'm feeling sick,' I lied, hoping the person couldn't hear my stomach growl.

The lamp didn't move. Blinking, I saw the outline

of a steward. He grabbed my arm. 'All steerage must be in the hold at night. Ship's orders.'

I tried to twist free but he held on firm.

'Find yourself a bucket to be sick in. There's plenty down there.'

He dragged me towards a hatch. With his free hand he flung it open. Heat, noise, the smell of dinners and damp clothing all rose up into my face.

'In you go,' said the steward, pushing me. 'And stay there.'

Above my head, the hatch slammed shut. A bolt slid across it. My spirits sank. This was my lot until morning.

Uneasily, I climbed down into the hold. The air was close and sour. And *snakes alive*, the noise! Up on deck, the engines were loud. Down here in the belly of the ship, the clunking, droning din seemed to drill inside my skull. I wondered how I'd stand it all night.

Yet people were getting ready to sleep. There were bunks along the sides and down the middle of the hold. I'd never seen so many beds all in one place. An old woman patted a place next to her.

'You look lost, dear,' she said.

'I ain't ever been on a ship before,' I said.

'Well, take a good long look. This is home for the next ten days.'

I shuddered.

'There's nothing a night's sleep won't cure,' she said. 'Come on, up you get.'

Grateful, I joined her on the hard wooden bunk. She even covered me with part of her blanket, which smelled of lavender and made me sad again for Jasper, Pip and the wagon we all shared. The rolling of the ship sent many folks off to sleep. Plenty more were poor sailors. Despite what the steward had said, there weren't many buckets. And once they'd filled up, folks had to use the floor. The smell was ripe.

All through the night the puking never stopped. Nor did the drone of the engines. When my eyes grew heavy at last, I dreamed of thunder. Each time I woke up gasping for air. My hand went straight to my shift and the red scrap underneath. Soon as I felt it, I knew the storm wasn't real. The ship sailed smoothly onwards.

*

At first light, the hatches were opened again. The air came in sharp and cold. Quick as you like, I was back up that ladder. We were now sailing in open sea. Behind us, the ship left a white trail across the water, and high above us, gulls still screeched. The wind had picked up a little. It helped clear my head, though the engine noise still rang in my ears.

More people emerged from steerage to empty their pails over the side. And then came the breakfasts of cake and hard biscuits. It was agony to watch people eating, knowing I'd no food myself. The old lady with the blanket might've shared what she had, but it didn't seem right to ask. I headed to the nearest gate. Locked, of course. So was the one on the other side of the ship.

Locked, locked, locked.

My frustration grew. There had to be a way through these gates. I went to kick the blasted thing. Then stopped.

A lone first-class passenger was up on deck. He was staring out to sea. He didn't have a hat on, and even though I wasn't sure it was him, I pressed my face against the bars of the gate.

'Mr Wellbeloved, sir?' I called. 'Mr Wellbeloved?'

The wind was strong. He didn't hear me. I tried again.

'Sir? Over here! Mr Wellbeloved!'

He didn't look up. Yet the more I studied him, the surer I was. This man was tall and slender, with jet-black hair. His side whiskers were pointed in the same unusual way.

I started waving frantically. 'Over here! Please! Sir!'

He glanced my way. Just once. Then he turned and went back inside.

I couldn't believe it. *So close and yet so far!* I shook the gate. Kicked it. Cussed at it.

The noise brought a steward running.

'Oi! What are you playing at?'

I froze.

'Get away from that gate, d'you hear me?'

I turned round. His shiny-buttoned chest blocked my path. It was the same gruff steward from last night.

'Ticket,' he said, holding out his hand.

I stared at it blankly.

'Ticket,' he said again. 'I've had enough of your mucking about.'

My heart plummeted. I was stuck. Well and truly. Behind me was the gate. In front was all silver buttons and dark wool coat.

'My nanna's got it,' I lied, 'and she's still asleep in the hold.'

He squared his shoulders. I could tell he wasn't buying it.

'We'd best go and find her then, hadn't we?' he said, and his big hand came down heavily on my shoulder.

Think, Louie, think. But my brain was whirling too fast. And he was dragging me back towards the hatch.

'I say! Stop at once!' cried a voice behind us.

The steward halted. Ever so slowly he turned, dragging me with him. Standing behind the gate was a gentleman wearing a very tall top hat.

'Mr Wellbeloved! Oh sir! It *is* you!' I cried.

The steward let me go. I rushed at the gate. Never was I so glad to see anyone.

'Oh sir! I must talk to you! It's urgent! Please, sir, you see . . .'

Mr Wellbeloved put a gloved finger to his lips. 'Not now,' he said. He turned his attention to the steward. 'This child is with me.'

'Then how come she's over here and you're over there?'

'My good fellow,' Mr Wellbeloved said, in a way that meant the opposite, 'let's not make a fuss. I will pay her passage and take custody of her. Now kindly open the gate.'

He gave the steward something; I didn't see what. But it was enough to put a smile on his face.

*

Within minutes I was sat in the dining saloon. The other passengers stopped eating. You'd have thought they'd never seen a girl before. *Let them stare,* I thought, for I never did mind being looked at. I even flashed a smile, though no one smiled back.

All the while, Mr Wellbeloved sat opposite me, chin resting on his hands. He smiled with his eyes, like something amused him. Perhaps it was my stomach, growling for all to hear. It was hard to concentrate on anything with dish after dish of food being carried past our table. So I was glad when he told me to order from the menu.

Then Mr Wellbeloved sat back in his chair. 'So, tell me,' he said, crossing his legs. 'What's this urgent matter you have to discuss with me, Louisa?'

I tensed up. No one called me Louisa. *Ever.*

His eyes were pale grey with dark rings around the coloured part. They made me think of wolves. I remembered what Mr Chipchase had said, about him not being all he seemed.

'Where's Gabriel?' I said suddenly. 'Is he all right?'

Visions of him locked in a cabin or tied to a chair sprang into my head.

Mr Wellbeloved smiled, this time with his mouth. 'He's very well, don't you fret. You'll see him soon enough.'

Relieved as I was, I felt myself go red. He'd seen my concern for Gabriel and it amused him.

Before I could say more, a silver domed plate was placed before me. Underneath it were eggs, kidneys, bacon. I ate fast. Mr Wellbeloved watched with raised eyebrows. And once I was finished, and had my cup refilled with hot chocolate for the second time, I put my elbows on the table. I was ready.

'I want to perform on the high wire,' I said. 'I *have* to perform. It's in my bones.'

I almost told him about Blondin and my scrapbook. But it felt a bit too private under that wolfish gaze. And I reckoned I could do this on my own merits.

'I have a very real talent, sir.'

He didn't say anything, but his eyes never left my face.

'I came after you because . . .' I faltered. 'I want this chance more than anything. America would be an absolute dream for me. You saw me that night at Chipchase's . . . I am good, sir, aren't I?'

He tilted his chin. Was it a 'yes'? I couldn't tell.

'So, you see, I think you chose the wrong person for your show. I'm here to ask you to reconsider.'

He stayed silent for a long moment. Then he said, 'I expected you to climb that locked gate, Louisa.'

'Pardon?'

I wished he'd call me Louie.

'Nothing will stand in your way. You've got guts. I admire that in a person.'

'Oh . . . right . . . well, ta very much.'

For someone I barely knew, he seemed to know me rather well. It made me think of Miss Lilly's cards, which had also seen inside me. It all felt a bit odd.

'Why didn't you choose me, then?' I said.

His eyes twinkled. 'Who says I haven't?'

I stared at him. Had he changed his mind? 'What are you saying, sir?'

'Nothing yet.'

He was toying with me. It was too much. My patience snapped. 'Please give me the chance, sir! Let me be your star turn! You won't regret it, I promise!'

His hand went up to silence me. 'Sometimes, Louisa, you have to wait patiently for gates to open.'

'But Gabriel doesn't want . . .' I stopped.

Stood in the doorway was Gabriel Swift. He wore a fresh suit of clothes and his hair flopped over his cheek. He looked surprisingly well.

'Gabriel!' I cried, jumping to my feet.

His face fell in horror. 'Louie . . . why are *you* here?'

CHAPTER 20

After breakfast we went to cabin 12A.

'Make yourselves at home,' said Mr Wellbeloved, though he didn't take off his hat.

The cabin was tiny for three of us. It was like being sardines in a box. Gabriel fidgeted so much our elbows kept bumping. Truth told, I was on edge myself. If only Mr Wellbeloved would change his mind, then we'd all be happy. Though for that I supposed I'd have to wait.

'We'll get a bed put in here for you,' Mr Wellbeloved said, opening a side door. Another tiny room led off it. 'The green trunk contains clothes. Select yourself something . . .' his eyes ran over me, '. . . appropriate for the upper deck.'

'Thank you, sir!'

First a fine breakfast, now new clothes. Things didn't seem *that* bad. Mr Chipchase had painted a right dark picture. Yet Mr Wellbeloved was actually being kind.

The tiny space was a dressing room of sorts. The trunk sat open on the floor, tissue paper spilling out over the sides. I knelt down and started rummaging till I was elbow deep in lace and silks. These weren't like circus clothes. The colours were pale, not bright, the skirts long, not short. And there wasn't a sequin or feather in sight. These were towners' clothes, *fine* towners' clothes. I'd never worn anything like them.

Outside, the wind had got up. The ship rolled, making the water slosh about in the basin on the washstand. I washed in it quick, then tried on a dress. It was pale blue with little buttons down the front, and it fitted snug as a glove. Yet stood before the mirror I hardly knew myself. The girl staring back looked so *dull*, as if her greatest dream was to sit in a parlour doing cross stitch. The frock wanted for a bright feather or extra ruffles on the sleeves, and the skirts were too long to walk in. Perhaps another of these dresses might suit me better. There were plenty to choose from, and they were all in my size. And all brought on board ship in Mr Wellbeloved's luggage.

My head began to spin. Mr Wellbeloved was travelling to America with a young man. And I might've been wrong, but Gabriel didn't look like the type to wear frocks.

So why bring them with him?

It was quite a coincidence.

There was a knock and the door opened.

'Perfect,' said Mr Wellbeloved, taking in my new look.

I forced a smile. 'Thank you, sir.'

'And were the other clothes suitable?'

I hesitated. He read my face. 'Ah! Not fancy enough for you, eh?'

'No, sir, it's not really that. It's just that . . . well . . .' I couldn't hide my doubts. 'Gabriel's the performer you chose, so it's . . . well, *surprising* to find all these girls' clothes here. I can't imagine they were meant for him.'

He didn't say anything. I fiddled with the buttons on my dress as I felt his eyes bore into me. Then he laughed. Head back, a flash of gold teeth showing. Once, in a sideshow, I'd seen a caged tiger yawn; I was reminded of it now.

'Think about it, Louisa,' was all he said.

*

I did think about it. So much that my head hurt. The best cure was being up on deck, leaning over the rail as the sea churned below. The salty spray turned my new frock stiff and my hair escaped its pins, though I didn't much care. In the end, only one idea made sense: Mr Wellbeloved had chosen Gabriel by a whisker. The clothes had been packed just in case he'd gone for me, and he'd not had time to remove them. It sounded a fair bet, and it made me feel easier. For if it really had been so close, surely he'd agree to swap us over. He didn't *seem* to mind my being here. Quite the reverse, in fact.

Unlike Gabriel.

His fine manners had deserted him. Clearly, he didn't want me to take his place at all. In fact, he seemed jealous. Perhaps Mr Wellbeloved had promised him great things in America, and now he did want the glory after all. Me turning up had scuppered his plans; I'd seen as much in his face. It made me want to shake him.

Or perhaps I should be feeling guilty. No. I couldn't manage that. Not long ago Gabriel had come to *my* circus, taken a role that should've been mine. This was what I kept reminding myself.

*

By late afternoon the storm had set in proper. Most people had taken to their cabins, and I found Gabriel in ours. He was stretched out on his bunk, but seeing me he sat up sharpish.

'You ain't very pleased I'm here, are you?' I said.

He got up off the bed.

'No you don't.' I blocked his way out. He sat down again. 'Not till you tell me what's going on.'

Gabriel held his head in his hands. I supposed he was seasick, for he did look frightful pale. 'What are you doing here, Louie?' he said. 'You stowed away, didn't you?'

'Might've.'

'Why?'

I sighed. Had he really forgotten that night at Littleton, when he'd been too terrified to perform and I'd brought the house down? *Me*. Not him.

It was time for plain talking. 'Mr Wellbeloved was going to *choose* one of us that night.' I stressed the word. 'Then, despite the fact that you'd run away once, and you didn't want to go with him, he did *choose* you. It doesn't make sense.'

Gabriel shook his head. 'You shouldn't be here,' he said bleakly.

'But don't you see? That night at Chipchase's, this seemed like the last thing you wanted. Yet for me it was a dream come true. I believed he might choose

194

me – it would've been best for both of us. I even told Jasper all about it!'

Only now I felt daft. It was obvious I'd got the wrong end of the stick about Mr Wellbeloved's intentions. And Gabriel's for that matter. 'So why *are* you here? After what happened. After you . . .' I hesitated.

' . . . seized up. Got stage fright. Couldn't do it.' Now he glared at me.

'I didn't mean it like that.'

Neither of us spoke. Outside, the wind raged. Rain lashed against the porthole window. It suited my spirits, which had sunk to a new low. I'd wanted to help Gabriel, not fight with him. It seemed I'd mucked that up too.

Then Gabriel said, 'You still haven't answered my question. Why are you here?'

'To change Mr Wellbeloved's mind. If I get the American job, you'll be able to go home. And we'll both be happy.'

I didn't mention Mam – that was family business, best kept private. Jasper doubted I'd find her, and he was probably right.

Gabriel smiled weakly. 'Mr Wellbeloved won't just swap us, Louie. Things aren't that simple.'

He wasn't jealous of me, I saw that now. He didn't sound anything like a person wanting glory.

'Let's wait and see,' I said.

'It won't do any good.' He clasped his hands together, flexing his fingers. 'I broke my contract by coming to Chipchase's. That's why he followed me.'

'Oh.' My stomach dropped. 'Heck.'

In the circus world, broken contracts were bad with a capital B. Ned had told me about it, tales of battered legs and poisoned horses. I didn't know whether to be cross or sorry. But I did finally understand. No wonder Gabriel was so uptight.

A sudden wave hit the ship. I staggered sideways. 'Can I sit down?'

Gabriel shifted up to make room for me. I dropped down heavily beside him.

'So, Mr Wellbeloved won't agree to it,' he said again.

'Well, he ain't exactly thrown me overboard.'

'Not yet, no.'

I looked sideways at him. 'What d'you mean by that?'

'He's not a man to be crossed.'

'He's been all right to me,' I said, gesturing at my dress.

'No one says no to Mr Wellbeloved and gets away with it.'

'But I want him to say *yes*!'

'Be careful what you wish for, that's all.'

Without meaning to, I glanced at his neck. Those marks were still there, though by now they'd gone purple. Quickly, I looked away.

'He's planning something for America. Something very, very big,' Gabriel said.

'Tell me.'

'That's all I know. You should have stayed at Chipchase's, Louie. He made you a showstopper. Wasn't that what you wanted?'

It was.

Yet, now the idea of America had taken hold, nothing else was enough. I couldn't just go home and forget all about it.

'It took me years to get that showstopper part,' I said. 'And I still don't understand why Mr Chipchase changed his mind so sudden. Mostly, he just holds me back. Still wants to, I reckon, even though he knows I've got talent.'

For that was how it felt. There was always some reason why I *couldn't* do things, rather than why I *could*. Yet how to explain it to a boy who was scared?

The very things he feared, I loved with all my being.

And there was my mam. The hope of finding her had taken root too. It wasn't about to go away, though I'd no idea where to start looking.

'Well, I'm glad I'm here,' I said. 'But Mr Wellbeloved *is* a bit strange, ain't he? And I do wish he'd take that blasted hat off sometimes.'

'Louie,' said Gabriel. 'He *never* takes that hat off.'

Which struck me as odd. Because on deck this morning he *was* hatless. Yet when he came to the gate to speak to me the hat was definitely on again.

'Maybe it's his lucky hat,' I said, though it didn't sound likely. Someone as rich as Mr Wellbeloved had luck enough already.

'Well, he's certainly attached to it,' said Gabriel.

'And to you. He doesn't want to let you go in a hurry either.'

Gabriel stiffened. 'I told you. I broke my contract. Just leave it, can't you?'

'All right! No need to snap!'

We fell into uneasy silence. It wasn't like Gabriel to be touchy. Mid-thought, my hand went to my shift strap. My fingers stopped. Mam's heart wasn't there. I prodded my sleeve right down to the wrist; not there either. Bewildered, I scanned the cabin.

'What have you lost?' asked Gabriel.

I crouched down to look under the bunk. Just packing cases and dust, nothing else. Dizzily, I stood up. 'A piece of red cloth shaped like a heart. It's important.'

Gabriel got off the bunk as I thumped pillows, shook out blankets. No sign of it.

'It must be here somewhere,' I said, growing hot.

'We'll find it, don't worry.'

He didn't ask questions, like whose heart was it and why was it so special. Not like Ned, who'd push and push until he got an answer. It was some relief. Certain things were best left alone until you were ready; Gabriel understood that about me at least.

While he checked the cabin, I searched the dressing room. By now I was close to frantic. I looked everywhere: my old clothes, the trunk full of new ones. Then we went back up on deck, and came down again. We retraced every single step but found nothing. The heart had vanished into thin air.

CHAPTER 21

And so I turned gloomy. Miss Lilly's cards had predicted difficult times. Now that one more bad thing had happened, I feared others would come fast on its heels. All without Mam's heart to bring me luck. I pined for Pip too. It was odd to wear new clothes with not a single dog hair on them. And I thought often of dear Jasper and prayed he was healing well.

Meantime, the weather grew colder. Icebergs the size of houses drifted past us. Each night they groaned like beasts, then at sunrise they turned the colour of the sky. The ship had to slow down to sail around them because, Gabriel said, an iceberg was much bigger below the water, and that what you saw wasn't even half the story. The image troubled me more than I'd have liked.

Then, three evenings later, there was to be dancing in the ballroom. By now I was ready for a bit of fun. Mr Wellbeloved still hadn't made clear his intentions.

He spent most of his days sending telegrams and pacing about like a panther. This plan of his – whatever it was – had clearly fired him up. It didn't help steady me down.

'Oh, do tell us what you're planning, sir,' I'd asked more than once.

'Patience, Louisa,' he'd always reply.

So it was a joy to think only of dancing. I chose my frock with extra care, a dark green silk one with long ruffled skirts. A quick scamper up and down the passage told me I'd be able to dance a polka in it. And it was a beauty of a frock; its colour set off my bright hair a treat.

'Will you dance?' I asked Gabriel as the band struck up their first tune.

No one else had yet got to their feet. The empty dance floor stretched before us. High above it was a domed glass ceiling, the night sky all black against it. The room itself seemed to glitter. There were lamps and mirrors on every wall, and wherever you looked champagne glasses caught the light. Around the edges of the dance floor people sat in armchairs, talking loudly. The whole place was abuzz. And so was I.

'I'm supposed to ask you, Louie,' said Gabriel.

He looked dashing in evening tails and a white necktie. Mr Wellbeloved, who sat with us, wore the same. Though because he'd kept his hat on the effect was more dramatic. More showy.

I didn't see the point in sitting down just to stand up again. So I grabbed Gabriel's hand and pulled him to his feet. 'Thank you, I'd love to dance,' I said.

His face lit up with a grin. I'd not seen him smile for days, and I'd missed it. Though I hadn't missed Mr Wellbeloved's pale eyes. I felt them now, burning into my back.

'Come on, then,' I said, eager to be off.

Gabriel resisted. 'No, let's do it properly.' He put a hand on my shoulder, the other supporting my fingers.

'Ready?'

I nodded.

He counted us in. 'One and two, three and four.'

It made me giggle. 'I *can* dance. I'm not a complete ninny.'

In reply, he swung me round so fast my hair whipped my cheeks. We set off across the room, Gabriel leading, me going backwards. We moved light as clouds. At the end of the floor, Gabriel stopped. Releasing my hand, I turned under his arm. He was still smiling. I didn't look anywhere else; I didn't want to. Yet I felt everyone's eyes on us now. It sent little shivers right down to my feet.

'Let's show 'em!' I said, as Gabriel took my hand again.

At the right beat, we set off again in a polka. We went faster now, skipping and turning at dizzying speed. The violins matched our pace. Round and round the floor we went. Our feet moved in perfect time. I laughed for the sheer joy of it. Gabriel looked awful happy too, as if he was surprised by how good it felt.

'A bit more?' I said, as we broke from our hold.

He nodded eagerly.

'Watch me.'

I didn't go back into his arms. This time, I hitched up my skirts and skipped on the spot in a jig. Then I spun round, once, twice. The music took hold of me as I danced round the floor. Arms raised, I felt my hair fly outwards. I imagined myself not on board a fancy ship but at home dancing before the flames of a campfire. The heat of it glowed inside me. I didn't want to stop.

But Gabriel touched my arm.

'Shall we?' he said, holding out his hands.

I took them. Facing each other, we crossed our arms at the wrists.

'Lean back,' he said. 'Just shuffle your feet on the spot.'

As I did so, we started to spin. We went slowly at first. Then our feet got faster. And faster. The ballroom whizzed by in a blur of lights. Gabriel's grin spread huge across his face. I'd lost count of the music now. All I felt was the whirling in my head.

Eventually, the music slowed. We came to a dizzy stop.

'Thank goodness that's over!' said someone within earshot. 'They dance like savages, not children!'

Gabriel caught my eye. We pulled faces and sniggered behind our hands. Better savage than dullard any day of the week.

Other couples had now taken to the floor. Their polkas were slower, lumpier attempts than ours. And they kept cutting across us, shooting cold looks our way as they passed. It was time to sit down.

Back at our table, Mr Wellbeloved was statue-still. He didn't speak, though I sensed he had something to say. I gulped down some water and flopped into a chair. Gabriel sat opposite me. His face was flushed with heat.

'That was quite a spectacle,' said Mr Wellbeloved in a voice so quiet I had to lean forward to catch it.

I sat back. *Oh*. He didn't seem pleased. Gabriel wasn't smiling now either.

'We were just having a bit of a lark, sir,' I said.

'Indeed, I saw. So did the rest of the upper deck.'

I looked across at Gabriel. *Say something, then*, I willed him, but he stared miserably at his feet. I crossed my arms. So, we should've danced like carthorses, should we? At least then we'd have blended in. But what showstopper in their right mind would want that?

The music's jaunty beat began to grate on me. I didn't think I'd dance again tonight. I got to my feet. 'I've a headache,' I lied, 'so I'll say goodnight.'

Gabriel stood up fast. 'I'm coming too.'

'Wait a moment,' Mr Wellbeloved said. 'You seem to have taken offence.'

I stared at him, confused.

'It was a compliment,' he said. 'Your polka might not have been to everyone's taste, but every single person in this room was watching you.'

'Oh,' I said. 'That's different, then.' I admit I felt rather pleased.

'There's something between you two. You have a . . . what shall we say . . . a chemistry. A connection,' Mr Wellbeloved said.

Suddenly, I couldn't meet Gabriel's eye.

'We'd be foolish not to put that connection to good use,' Mr Wellbeloved said. 'Very foolish indeed.'

Gabriel breathed in sharply. His eyes closed in a long, painful blink.

'What d'you mean by that, sir?' I said.

'Think about it, Louisa.'

My brain went blank. I'd no idea what he meant.

Then I felt it in my belly, a cold hard sense that something wasn't right. Oh no. He wouldn't: *or would he?*

'Sir,' I said, struggling to stay calm. 'That night at Chipchase's you said the offer was for one of us only. So I'll ask you again: give me the job. And let Gabriel go home.'

'Louie . . .' Gabriel tried to protest.

I kept on. 'Please, sir! A dance is one thing, but the tightrope's something else. It ain't right to put him through it, not when I'm so willing.'

Mr Wellbeloved sat back in his seat and crossed his legs. 'Did I really say the offer was just for one of you?'

'You did, sir! You know you did!'

He didn't answer. His face gave nothing away either.

For six more days and nights, Mr Wellbeloved kept us dangling. Then a red light appeared on the horizon. Someone on deck cried, 'There's Halifax!' and a cheer went up. Not from me. The sight of land made my heart thud, for it meant we'd soon know our fate.

The very next morning we sailed down a channel busy with boats. Two pilots guided us in to New York harbour, which looked so different from Liverpool. The buildings here were low and mostly made of wood, and the air had a tang to it, like the sea mixed with tree sap.

An hour or two later, we arrived in dock. After being checked for fever, we finally set foot on dry land. The whole world tipped sideways until my legs got used to it. The docks were thick with passengers just off the ship, and pedlars selling oranges and onions, and others offering rooms for the night, all hollering to be heard.

And then something quite extraordinary happened: a sudden surge in the crowd knocked Mr Wellbeloved's hat off. It fell from his head onto the cobbles. Hatless, he seemed to be shielding his right ear.

'Move along,' said a woman, pushing into me as I stopped and stared.

Next time I looked, his hat was firmly back in place.

*

Mr Wellbeloved didn't let go of his hat rim again until we were on a train, heading north. That Gabriel and me were both still here revealed something of his plans. In the seat opposite mine, Gabriel's fingers drummed against his knees. And he seemed so far away, so dazed, it was near impossible to talk to him. In turn, it rattled me. Me, who should've been thrilled just to be here. Yet my dream was his nightmare. It made the whole thing so bittersweet it was becoming hard to bear.

As it was, we soon left the city behind us, passing forests and grass plains far bigger and greener than any back home. It all looked the same after a while. If my mam was anywhere out there I'd sooner find a needle in a hay barn. Eventually, my eyelids grew heavy. It was then Mr Wellbeloved cleared his throat, making me jump in my seat.

'Louisa, Gabriel,' he said, 'I have a proposition for you both.'

My mouth went awful dry. I glanced at Gabriel; he was fidgeting with his jacket sleeves.

'You will perform on the high wire,' he said, looking straight at me. 'And, I promise you will take America by storm.'

My jaw dropped. At last. The words I'd been dying to hear. 'Oh thank you, sir!' I gasped.

But he'd already moved on to Gabriel. 'Both of you.'

The excitement went dead.

'I'll pay handsomely,' he said. 'You'll go home with fame and fortune.'

No one spoke. The world flashed by outside the window and suddenly it was hard to breathe. As Mr Wellbeloved shifted in his seat, Gabriel shrank back in his. His face was white.

I began to shake all over.

This was wrong. *All wrong*.

'Sir, it didn't go well last time, not with the two of us,' I pleaded. 'It'd be much easier to just take me.'

Mr Wellbeloved looked surprised. 'But of course it would. That's why I want you both.'

It took a second to understand what he was saying. As a performer, I knew the risks. And I did my best to stay safe. This was different. It wasn't about Gabriel's contract – or not only that. This was about pushing things *beyond* the limit.

And he wasn't finished yet.

'You'll be Master Blondin and Little Miss Blondin, after the Great Blondin himself.'

Taking a deep breath, I said, 'Does it have to be Blondin?', for it didn't sit well with me, not since Sharpfield, when my hero had fallen a long way short.

'Yes.' Mr Wellbeloved fixed me with his piercing eyes. 'It fits perfectly. No other name will do.'

Slowly, painfully, it dawned on me. My heart felt ready to punch through my ribs. 'So we've come here to be like Blondin?' I said.

'Exactly right. Just like Blondin. Except there'll be two of you.'

Blondin had come to America to do one thing. A remarkable, death-defying thing that I'd pored over pictures of for as long as I could remember. At last, I understood Mr Wellbeloved's plan.

My head filled up too much, too fast. Mr Wellbeloved had bought me dresses, paid my passage. He was my ticket to better things. I'd wanted this so badly. Yet his plan was madness.

'It's Niagara Falls, isn't it?' I said. 'You want us both to cross Niagara Falls.'

This wasn't a *WHIFF of death* show.

It wasn't even close.

No, this had the very *STENCH of death* to it.

Mr Wellbeloved smiled, showing his teeth. 'Yes, my dear, I do. And you shall.'

✳ SECOND ACT ✳

Wellbeloved's Fabulous Funambulists

CHAPTER 22

I awoke in a big brass bed. It was morning. Sun beat against the still-drawn curtains, making the room feel stifling hot. A drumming sound filled my head, and for a second I thought I was back on the ship in steerage. Only I wasn't, I was in a fancy bedchamber.

We'd travelled into the night to reach Niagara Falls. The noise hit me as soon as I'd stepped off the train. It sounded like distant thunder or the rumbling belly of a horse. A cab took us through dark streets to a house signposted, 'Mrs Franklin's Lodgings', where Mr Wellbeloved said he always stayed. For Gabriel and me, he'd booked the rooms either side of his own. This was where I found myself now.

The bed was too big for me alone. It needed Pip crawling up it to lick me good morning. And the room itself, all dried flowers and frills, didn't feel right either. What I'd give to see a painted chair or a hand-knitted blanket. Or to smell lapsang tea as it steamed in my cup. All at once I felt a great ache for home.

I'd not even Mam's taffeta heart to comfort me. It seemed an omen for everything I felt, especially in my dream of finding Mam. Where was the empress Miss Lilly's cards had promised? The only person watching over me was Mr Wellbeloved, and that didn't feel much like help. My lip started trembling. Then came tears, great fat ones dripping off my cheeks and onto the pillow.

Eventually, I sat up and rubbed my eyes. So far I'd not helped Gabriel much, and though I was sorry, it shouldn't make me lose sight of why I was here. Most of all, I wanted to go home proud and happy. And I wanted it to be soon.

Getting out of bed, I threw open the windows. Instantly, the growl of the Falls became a roar. I stepped onto a little balcony, blinking in the sunshine. The ravine lay about two hundred yards ahead. Trees gave way to bare rock and then, far below, the river ran white and furious. The sight made my stomach twist.

Clear as day, I saw the headline: HORROR AND DISGUST AS CHILDREN PLUMMET TO THEIR DOOM. And back at Chipchase's, I imagined Jasper reading the newspapers and wondering who this Master Blondin and Little Miss Blondin were. Perhaps even Ned would too. Knife sharp, I felt another pang for home. It almost made me turn and run. Yet something held me to the spot.

My eyes followed the river upstream, past the big steel bridge that spanned the gorge. A fluttering started in my belly. I knew this scene from the pictures in my scrapbook. Dotted among the trees were more houses joined by dirt roads, and then bigger buildings that might've been factories or mills. Further on, a mist hung over the water. As I craned my neck, I saw what looked like a park with tents in it.

Further on still, *blimey*, there they were, Niagara Falls themselves. Or rather, two waterfalls. The smaller American Falls were on this side of the ravine. Up ahead were Horseshoe Falls, the water like a wall curving from one bank to the other. The sound was never-ending. A rushing, rumbling noise like it was inside your skull. None of it felt quite real. I was spellbound.

And in that moment it all made sense; why Blondin had walked Niagara Falls, and why we would too. It wasn't just the glory of performing for the crowds, or the money. It was more about taking their breath away. Doing something extraordinary. Making punters forget their woes for a few measly minutes, and being sure they'd never forget you.

But for Gabriel it wasn't like that. He'd nearly come to grief that night at Chipchase's. To freeze up over Niagara Falls, with no wooden platform ten steps behind, would be horrifying. It was too risky – for both of us. Mr Wellbeloved *had* to change his mind. Yet no one said no to him, so Gabriel reckoned. And I was beginning to see what he meant.

I went back inside and dressed quickly. Just as I reached the door, I heard voices in the hallway. One was a woman's with a strange, lilting accent. The other belonged to Mr Wellbeloved.

'Kindly let me pass, before this water goes cold,' said the woman. It was Mrs Franklin, who owned the lodgings.

'Don't you have a maid for that?' said Mr Wellbeloved.

'She's busy with all these guests arriving for your show.'

'Then hire another one.'

'I can't just do that.'

'You can if I tell you to.'

'Please let go of my wrist,' Mrs Franklin said. Then came a sharp cry. 'You're hurting me!'

'I need to trust you,' he said in a low hiss, 'with the girl. You know very well who she is.'

Girl? Did he mean me? I crouched near the keyhole to hear more.

A rustle of skirts. Another squeal. I flinched.

'I've trusted you this far,' Mr Wellbeloved said. 'Don't let me down now.'

There was more whispering, then retreating footsteps. I guessed they'd both gone.

Then came a knock at the door. I leaped away from it quick.

Mr Wellbeloved didn't wait to be asked in. He shut the door behind him and slammed a jug of hot water down on the washstand. 'So, my dear, have you worked it out yet?'

'Worked out what, sir?'

'We've met before, haven't we?'

I shuddered like someone had walked over my grave. *Sharpfield*. So he had remembered.

'As soon as I saw you, I knew,' he said.

'Knew what?'

Mr Wellbeloved studied me closely, head on one side. 'Your hair. It's quite unusual, don't you think?'

Anyone else saying it and I'd have grinned and said

thank you. Instead, I tucked my hair behind my ears with a scowl.

'Mr Chipchase didn't like it,' I said. 'He made me cover it up, often as not.'

Mr Wellbeloved looked amused. 'Did he now?'

But it wasn't funny, not to me. It didn't feel right to talk of Mr Chipchase either, and I wished I'd kept quiet. I tried to reach the door again, but he put an arm out to stop me.

'Louisa,' he said. 'Listen to me. It means nothing that I chose Gabriel. I could've chosen anyone, just as long as I chose someone over you.'

I stared at him. What on earth did he mean? The man was clearly warped.

Then I remembered what he'd said about the ship's gate and me climbing it.

'I knew you'd come anyway,' he said. 'And the harder I made it for you, the more you'd want it. Like I said, you've got guts.'

It sounded bizarre, yet it also made sense: the trunk full of dresses, the offering to pay my passage. It was as if he'd been expecting me. I shuddered again. What kind of person would plan such a thing?

'I needed to know you'd be up to the task,' he said. 'Crossing the Falls isn't for the faint-hearted.'

'So why make Gabriel do it?'

Mr Wellbeloved folded his arms. 'Gabriel is my performer, Louisa. He does as I say, and that's final.'

I opened my mouth to plead. Then shut it again. It was pointless. One look at those pale eyes and I knew the case was closed.

'The crowd must expect danger,' Mr Wellbeloved said. 'You know that as well as I do.'

I did. The *whiff of death*.

'Believe me, I know,' he said. 'Crossing Niagara was my dream once too.'

'*You* were a performer?'

'Indeed. Yet someone else crossed the Falls first.'

'Blondin,' I whispered.

'Indeed, Monsieur Blondin.' Mr Wellbeloved sneered at the name. 'Now it's your turn, and we must give the public something different. Something original.'

My head was spinning. What an odd way to do business. Not at all like Mr Chipchase; you knew where you were with him. With Mr Wellbeloved, everything was so ... well ... *twisted*.

'First we must eat,' he said.

Not that I had much appetite now. But I was

relieved when he finally opened the door. Halfway through it, he stopped.

'Ah, yes, I nearly forgot.' He reached inside his jacket and pulled something out. 'I do believe this is yours.'

He held out a clenched fist, turned it over and opened his fingers. Lying on his palm was my mam's red taffeta heart.

'Oh, sir! I hunted everywhere for this and thought I'd lost it!' I cried, taking it from him.

'It means a lot to you, I can see.'

'Yes . . . it's my . . .' I stopped.

He was staring at me queerly again. I didn't want to talk about Mam. She was my business, not his.

CHAPTER 23

The park I'd seen from my window was a pleasure garden. An hour later, the three of us were walking through it. Though it was still early the place was busy. Mr Wellbeloved marched us past rose bushes and sprawling green lawns where people strolled with their parasols or sat drinking tea. Tomorrow we'd be risking our lives for these strangers. That was circus for you; thrills and spills all the way.

What I hadn't reckoned on were the dogs. They were everywhere in the park: small ones on laps, big ones chasing sticks, even a terrier doing tricks with his ball. They all looked at their owners in that special way. It brought a lump to my throat; what I'd give to have Pip here with me now.

We took a cinder path through some trees. The river's roar grew louder till it was almost deafening. Finally, Mr Wellbeloved stopped.

'This is the point where you will cross the river,'

he yelled.

All I could see were workmen rigging up guy ropes and banging nails into a wooden platform. Once they'd moved aside, I saw properly. The gorge fell away just feet from where we stood. Spray from the river hung in the trees. The ground beneath us seemed to hum.

Just a few hundred feet further upstream were the Falls themselves. This close they took my breath away. They were, quite simply, walls of water. Churning, frothing, never-ending water. It was mesmerising.

And terrifying.

The rope was barely an inch wide. It stretched high above the ravine. On the other side, a thousand feet away, was Canada. And many, many feet below were rocks and raging water.

It was totally, completely crazy. Especially with two people, one of whom was petrified and likely not to make even the first step. Gabriel seemed to think so too. His face was frozen with fear.

A great wave of panic hit me. I felt suddenly, horribly sick.

Breathe, Louie. Be brave.

I moved away from Mr Wellbeloved and Gabriel.

I needed to gather myself. Saying the words helped. Mam's taffeta heart was safe inside my shift again; I touched it now. And as I did something strong rose up in me, beating back the fear. It wasn't crazy. Not if you trusted the tightrope. And I did, more than life itself. If only Gabriel could feel the same.

Once I'd rejoined the others, we walked back through the gardens. This time we took a different path, passing stalls selling coffee and roasted nuts. Mr Wellbeloved ushered us into a small striped tent, where tunics and tights awaited us. We were instructed to get changed and be ready for practice in five minutes.

My fingers shook so hard it was near impossible to get dressed at all. It took us both far longer than five minutes. Mr Wellbeloved was clearly irritated when we finally emerged.

'Sit!' he snapped, pointing to a bench nearby.

We sat. He stood before us, hands clasped behind his back.

'What's left of today is for practising,' he said. 'I want the same routine you did at Chipchase's.'

Gabriel's shoulders dropped in relief.

'The one you *should've* done,' he said. 'Not the cobbled together effort you eventually pulled off.'

I winced. 'In the circumstances, sir, I reckon we did pretty well.'

'*You* did, Louie,' Gabriel said bleakly. 'I was useless.'

'It wasn't perfect, I agree,' Mr Wellbeloved said. 'Tomorrow's show will be. Or else.'

Or else, what? I wanted to say. But he talked on, of timings and costumes, of posters and inviting the press. As we got up to leave I spoke quietly to Gabriel.

'Think only about the rope. Fill your head with it.'

He frowned. 'What do you mean?'

'It takes the fear away. You'll see.'

He nodded, though he didn't look convinced. His eyes had glazed over and he was chewing on the inside of his cheek. I wondered if he'd even heard me.

*

Yet Gabriel did notice the crowd. A hundred or so people had gathered to watch us practise on a rope set up in the park by Mr Wellbeloved's men. It was deliberately viewable from the main street, Portage Road; a little taster of things to come.

Gabriel straightened his shoulders and nodded to me. 'All set?'

'Certainly am.'

The fear was a distant thing. All I felt was a tingling in the soles of my feet. As we climbed our rope ladders Mr Wellbeloved warmed up the crowd. He wasn't quite Mighty Ned, but it still had the right effect.

'Watch and be amazed! Because tomorrow you'll see something even more extraordinary, performed by these two artists over Horseshoe Falls!'

A cheer went up.

The *stench of death*, I thought, putting on my best smile. Gabriel smiled too. The girls in the crowd all sighed at once.

'Are you ready?' I called down.

'Yes indeedy!' someone cried back.

'Then we'd be delighted to entertain you,' said Gabriel, bowing from the waist.

The girls giggled. I glanced at him myself: *goodness, how he'd livened up!*

It was infectious. The tingling in my feet grew until the magic took hold. I'd not felt this way since leaving England, and now that I did I was sure I could do anything. Flicking back my hair, I flexed my feet and rolled my shoulders. On the other side of the rope, Gabriel gave a little nod. I nodded back.

All set.

We did our routine from start to finish. All that mattered was the rope, reading its every twitch, every tremble as it lived beneath my feet. Gabriel played his part beautifully. This time we stepped around each other, and though the rope swayed we kept steady. He wrote me a letter, and I read it out loud, which made the girls sigh even more. There were walks to and fro, and we kept in the part where I lay down to sleep. It worked an absolute treat.

By the time we'd finished Gabriel was all lit up. And so was I.

'Crikey, Louie, that was . . . just . . .' he searched for the word.

'Magical?'

'Exactly!' He grinned. 'I did as you said, blocked out all the fear, and just focused on the rope.'

'It works, doesn't it? You can't think of the rope *and* be scared. It's impossible.'

'Then I'm cured! You're a miracle worker!'

'Glad to be of service!' I laughed, awful pleased. It wasn't the way I'd hoped to help Gabriel, but if he felt happier then so did I.

Once the crowd had moved off, we sat on the rope, dangling our legs. We chatted about our routine and how well it went and which were our favourite parts.

As we did so, my hopes began to rise. Perhaps Gabriel really could master his fear. Tomorrow, we'd perform our story above the Niagara Falls and it would be marvellous. Better even than Blondin.

Then Mr Wellbeloved came over. He stood directly beneath us, so I was looking down onto his hat.

'And the double somersault at the end, Louisa?' he said. 'Had you forgotten?'

My face fell. He wasn't expecting me to do that over the Falls, *was he*?

'Ah . . . you see . . . sir, well that was just a filler,' I stuttered. 'It ain't part of the normal routine.'

'It stays.'

But it had been a one-off. A spur of the moment grand finale to make up for Gabriel not taking part. I couldn't do it again.

'Sir, it ain't really . . .'

He glared up at me. Though he stood some ten feet below us, it still felt too close.

'Louisa,' he said. 'Do you want to go home a sensation?'

'Why yes, sir . . .'

His hand shot up and grabbed my ankle, yanking it once like a bell rope. 'Do you want to go home *at all*?'

' 'Course I do!'

'Good. Because you wouldn't want me to keep you here in America, would you?'

I stared at him in horror. 'You can't do that!'

'Can't I?'

He saw the fear in my face and let go of me, laughing.

'Think about it, Louisa,' he said.

I wished he'd stop saying that. I'd done little else recently other than ponder his strange ways. Now it was beginning to make me panic.

I'd only got to America because Mr Wellbeloved had paid my passage. I didn't have a penny of my own to get home again, and I couldn't stow away. Not after Niagara, which would make me a recognisable face. Without a ticket, I was stuck.

*

Once the crowd had gone, Mr Wellbeloved summoned us a ride home. I pretended to have another headache.

'I'd like to walk,' I said.

Mr Wellbeloved jabbed at the ground with his cane.

'Go with her, boy. Make sure she doesn't get *lost*,'

he said and took out his pocket watch. 'I'll expect you back by five.'

We watched as the carriage lurched away from us. Only when it was out of sight did Gabriel speak. 'He's suspicious,' he said as we set off up the hill. 'He thinks we might run away.'

'You *are* joking?'

'No. He knows we're not happy. He'll be keeping a close eye on us from now on.'

He was right. I wasn't happy. And if anyone was asking, there was a long list of reasons why.

I'd been star-struck, hadn't I? Back in England, I'd got on that train like a giddy halfwit. The reality wasn't all fancy frocks and hot chocolate at breakfast. There was another side to Mr Wellbeloved, and I didn't like it much. Better that I'd listened more to Mr Chipchase and to Jasper. Never mind even *trying* to find my mam. Yet what churned me up most was this threat of not going home. He'd found my weak spot all right. Except caring for something wasn't a weakness, not in my book. And I wasn't a quitter either.

CHAPTER 24

The sight of us walking along the main road in our tights and tunics certainly turned a few heads. What turned mine were the handbills stuck on every lamp post. 'NIAGARA FALLS', 'TIGHTROPE', 'DAZZLING' – all leaped out in big red letters. Underneath was the date: Friday 2 June.

Tomorrow.

Despite everything, I still felt a rush of excitement.

'Do *you* want to run away, then?' I asked, turning to Gabriel.

He'd seen the handbills too and was frowning.

'I tried that once before, if you recall?'

We walked on. Neither of us spoke. I'd grown almost used to Gabriel's silences.

Then, out of nowhere, I said, 'Back in England, did Mr Wellbeloved threaten you? Is that why you left?'

Gabriel sucked in his cheeks.

'Sorry,' I said. 'If you don't fancy saying...'

He shook his head. 'It's time I told somebody, I suppose. Mr Wellbeloved insisted we perform something against our wishes.'

'*We?*'

'My brother Albert and I. We walked the tightrope together, which, as you know, is difficult enough. Yet Mr Wellbeloved thought our routine was too tame.'

Mr Chipchase had said the same about Gabriel. Yet with two performers it surely had the *whiff of death* about it.

'What did he have in mind?' I asked.

Gabriel took a deep breath. 'He wanted us to carry chairs onto the rope ...'

'. . . And then sit in the middle and drink tea,' I finished. It was a Blondin trick: balancing a chair on the rope by only one chair leg and then sitting in it. It'd very nearly cost Blondin his life. And yet here the tables had been turned, and it was Mr Wellbeloved nicking the ideas.

'We had our concerns. But Albert was always braver than me. He said he'd try it first. But the balance wasn't right and he fell. I saw it all.'

'Oh Gabriel. That's awful.'

He stared ahead, dry-eyed. 'Yes, it was.' Then he blinked. 'He died right there in front of me. He was the only family I had left.'

I didn't know what to say, so I reached for Gabriel's hand and squeezed it, Jasper immediately in my mind. I'd never forget the sight of him falling through the air. How I'd gone to him not knowing if he was alive or dead. It still hurt like a punch on a bruise. And yet he *did* live. He *was* getting better.

Poor Gabriel. I could only imagine how dreadful he felt. 'I'm sorry,' I said.

He squeezed my fingers then let go; I found myself wishing he hadn't. Just to hold hands for a little while would've been comfort for us both.

We didn't talk of anything for a bit. We walked on, heads bowed, and I felt terrible for Gabriel. No wonder he was scared. No wonder he ran away. Why would he trust a tightrope after that? Just to even look at one would take courage.

I thought of Mr Wellbeloved; what had Mr Chipchase called him? *A gentleman of the shade.* He'd certainly been odd that night in Sharpfield. The way he'd looked at Blondin's daughter still gave me the shudders.

'So did you do the chair routine?' I asked Gabriel.

He gave a sort of half shrug. The sun had sunk below the trees, casting a shadow across his face.

'You said no one dared to stand up to Mr Wellbeloved. But did you?'

'I tried.'

He glanced up and down the street to check no one was watching. Then he stopped and rolled up one of his shirt sleeves. My hand went to my mouth.

'Oh heck!'

The skin on his forearm was slashed red with evil-looking scars. They started at the wrist and disappeared up beyond the elbow. The skin was quite newly healed.

'He whipped you,' I whispered. 'After all that had happened.'

'Horsewhipped,' said Gabriel. 'Eight lashes. Done in front of the other performers.'

I was stunned. Mr Chipchase didn't even *own* a horsewhip.

Gabriel covered his arm again. 'After Albert died, I wasn't fit to perform. Mr Wellbeloved saw it as shirking. Never mind that he still owed me wages from . . .' he faltered, '. . . before. But very conveniently, he forgot all about that and bullied me into performing. So when I saw the Chipchase advert, I just packed my bag and ran.'

I now felt rather shifty that I'd begrudged him the job. He'd needed it more than I had. And yet in the end, Mr Chipchase had made me a showstopper too, though he'd never really explained his decision.

We carried on up the hill. Mrs Franklin's white house was now in sight.

'That night when Mr Chipchase finally chose me, do you know why he changed his mind?' I asked.

'Money?' said Gabriel. 'I wasn't exactly pulling in the crowds by myself.'

'Nothing to do with Mr Wellbeloved, then?'

He looked at me. 'What do you mean?'

I didn't quite know. For so long I'd begged to perform, yet all I'd got for my pains was a second-rate buffer act. And even that I'd had to do in a clown's suit, with my hair tucked away. Then Ned told Mr Chipchase about a gent in a top hat asking questions. And by bedtime, I'd been made showstopper.

Why then, after all that time?

It was as if Mr Chipchase had been trying to hide me . . . and then suddenly . . . he wasn't.

'He knew Mr Wellbeloved was on the trail,' I said out loud.

Gabriel looked confused. 'Who did?'

'Mr Chipchase. Ned told him someone was after you, and he must've guessed.'

'So he made you showstopper because he knew I'd have to leave. That'll be the reason.'

I shook my head. 'He wasn't keen for me to stay showstopper. He said it brought too much trouble.'

'He was probably referring to those charity types.'

Do-gooders. Yet the night Mr Wellbeloved turned up, he'd not been sweating over *them*.

'Well, he didn't want me to come here, that's all I know,' I said, lifting my hair off my neck. It was hot still, despite the time of day.

'Perhaps he cares about you, Louie,' said Gabriel. 'Had you thought of that?'

I hadn't. Not from a man who was rarely civil to his own daughter.

As we walked, I mulled this over some more. Suppose Gabriel was right and Mr Chipchase did care. He'd taken me in as a baby, after all, or at least he'd let Jasper keep me. Perhaps there was more to him than his red face and short temper. Or perhaps he knew what Mr Wellbeloved was like. Either way, it unsettled me.

We'd almost reached our lodgings now. Just before Mrs Franklin's was a building with a porch out the front and 'Queenstown Stores and Post Office' painted above the door. A bunch of horses were tied to the porch posts, swishing their tails in the heat.

'Is that Mrs Franklin?' said Gabriel, shielding his eyes for a better look.

All I could see was horses' rumps. It was the sort of joke Ned might crack, and it did make me smile. After everything Gabriel had told me, I was glad he'd recovered a little.

'That's not nice, Gabriel,' I said, nudging him playfully.

Then I saw her myself, emerging from behind a grey horse. She was struggling to carry her basket. We went over to help.

'Let me carry that for you,' said Gabriel.

Mrs Franklin looked startled to see us. 'Goodness! I hardly recognised you both!'

Despite the heat, she looked pale. Her gaze slid over our tunics and tights. Then she sighed like a person in pain.

'It's all right. We've been performing,' I explained, for I decided I quite liked Mrs Franklin. She made nice breakfasts, and she had kind blue eyes. 'We don't normally go about the streets dressed like this.'

'Well, my dears, you certainly both look the part.'

She tried hard to smile but it came out as a muffled sob. 'I'm sorry. Do forgive me.'

'Please, let me take your basket,' said Gabriel gently.

'Oh, my dear,' she said. 'You are an angel.'

Handing it over, she winced. The fingers on her left hand were swollen and bruised.

'What happened to your hand?' I asked.

She pulled her sleeve down quickly. 'Oh, I'm clumsy. Don't mind me. I caught it in a door.'

She wasn't a very good liar. I bet I knew whose work this was; I'd heard them both this morning outside my bedroom. And what had Mr Wellbeloved said to her? Something about trust and her knowing who I was. Well, I'd never clapped eyes on her until last night. So I couldn't begin to think how she might know me.

No wonder Mrs Franklin's basket was heavy; it was full to the brim with vegetables. As Gabriel settled it into the crook of his arm, her eyes suddenly darted towards it. Mine did too. Stuck at an angle among the potatoes were some envelopes; I guessed about six. She snatched them up like they were hot and then stuffed them in her purse.

'Those are Mr Wellbeloved's,' she said, a bit too brightly.

Clearly, she didn't mean the potatoes.

CHAPTER 25

That night I couldn't sleep. I got up to open a window, but none of them would shift. Then something made me check the door. That too was locked. I rattled the handle but it held fast. I kicked the door hard.

He really was keeping a beady eye on us, then. Frustrated, I flopped down on the bed. What a fool I'd been to think Mr Wellbeloved held the answer to my dreams. Mr Chipchase had tried to warn me. So had Miss Lilly's cards. But I'd been too full of my own notions. I'd ignored all the signs.

Yet come what may, I'd see this through. That night in Sharpfield had taught me. Running away didn't solve things; it just put them off for a while. Mr Wellbeloved seemed to think only scared people ran. That's what Gabriel had done. And actually, all those years ago my mam had run from something too. Or *someone*.

I sat bolt upright.

Slowly, horribly, like ice dripping between my shoulder blades, I began to wonder. Did Mr Wellbeloved know something about . . . my mother?

I got to my feet, ran my fingers through my hair. No, of course he didn't. Why would he? It was a daft idea. My mam might be anywhere. Yet despite the heat of the room, my skin turned to gooseflesh.

He'd found the red taffeta heart. Or, I thought with a shiver, he'd taken it himself just to taunt me. Then there were the dresses bought especially for me, and that he deliberately hadn't chosen me so he could test the lengths I'd go to. He'd threatened Mrs Franklin, who might know who I was. And he'd commented on my red hair, which Mr Chipchase insisted I kept hidden. It was all mighty strange.

None of it was rock solid, but as hunches go, it was the only one I'd had so far. And it filled me with a sort of dread. Gabriel Swift had run away, yet Mr Wellbeloved had caught him. Mam had been running too when she abandoned me. *Please God*, if my hunch was right, that he'd never caught her. With a shudder I thought of his grip on my ankle today, and the threat that came with it. It was the very worse punishment to inflict on me, to keep me from the people I loved.

The air seemed to leave the room. I felt suddenly dizzy and had to sit down. After all these years, Mam had never come back for me. She'd promised; it was there in her letter. Mr Chipchase had expected it too. Now I realised it properly: something or *someone* really was stopping her. And I reckoned I might know who.

What I needed was proof.

I couldn't sit still. I got up again and paced the floor. *Think Louie, think.*

My brain went blank. Perhaps I was wrong about all this. It might just be nerves. What I needed was to talk to someone. But that alone was queer enough; whenever Jasper had tried, I'd clammed right up. Now I was bursting to tell. And with no Jasper here and no Ned, there was only one person for the job, someone who had earlier told me a painful secret of his own. Luckily he was just down the passageway in the next room but one.

No point trying the locked door. Instead, I went to the window and shook it. Once. Twice. Paint flaked off. The glass rattled. Then the lock began to lift from the frame. Another yank and it came off in my hand.

I eased myself out onto the balcony. The air was cool with its tang of the river. In the distance, the Falls roared on. Or perhaps it was my own pulse. A little shaft of light came from the next window along: Mr Wellbeloved's room. Beyond it was Gabriel's.

Flicking back my hair, I took a slow breath. Each balcony was about six feet apart. It looked easy enough. All I had to do was jump, then sneak past the lighted window. Below were bushes and trees, enough to break a fall. Not that I planned to fall anywhere.

After tying a knot in my nightshift hem, I climbed onto the railing. The handrail part was flat, about two inches wide. *Wide enough to stand on.* I felt with my feet. The metal was cold. My fingers touched the wall of the house for balance. Even a big stride wouldn't reach the next balcony. I had to jump. Mr Wellbeloved's balcony was cluttered with stupid plant pots, and I couldn't risk landing on one as it'd wake the whole town. His balcony had railings too, so I aimed for the handrail. It was my best shot. I counted down in my head. Felt my feet flex, my legs go tight. I pushed down, throwing myself forwards.

I hung in mid-air. Then my feet touched metal. Everything slowed down. I reeled backwards, then forwards, and didn't fall. Except I still had a lighted window to get past, and another balcony to jump to. From here it was clear that Gabriel's balcony wasn't six feet away; it was more like ten. I couldn't leap that far.

Mr Wellbeloved's curtains were open. I flattened myself against the building, his window at my right shoulder. Bit by bit, I peered inside; just one eye's worth of looking, the rest of me in shadow. He was sitting on a chair. I jerked back. *Had he seen me?* I waited for my heartbeat to slow. Then I looked again.

His room was bigger than mine. The bed was hung with drapes, and there were carpets on the floor. A far wall was covered in photographs. Opposite the bed was a dark wood wardrobe, its doors open to show shirts, jackets, scarves; far more than could fit in a travelling trunk. I supposed nowadays this room must count as his home.

Mr Wellbeloved got up from his chair. I shrank back, waited a moment, then had another look. He was leaning over his desk with a box open before him. He leafed through its contents at speed. Papers spilled out onto the floor. The faster he searched, the grimmer he looked. Then he stopped. He seemed to have found what he was after. In his hand was something red. It looked like fabric, all balled up. I peered closer, my breath misting up the glass. Now I couldn't see a thing.

In the end, I gave up looking. Tiptoeing to the other side of the balcony, I noticed Gabriel's window was in darkness. It really was too far to jump. There was nothing to swing from or grab hold of. Typical that now I was ready to talk about Mam, I couldn't get to the one person I trusted to listen.

I heard a window open.

'Who's out there?' It was Mr Wellbeloved.

I breathed in sharp. Leaped onto the handrail, stood flat against the wall. A shadow fell across the balcony.

'Louisa,' he said, a smile in his voice. 'Of course it's you.'

I bit my lip to stop me answering. *Drat him!* He'd locked me in on purpose, hadn't he? Not to stop me running, but to test me. He'd set the challenge and once again I'd seized it. I'd followed his trail of crumbs.

For a long, painful moment I didn't move. Mr Wellbeloved stayed at the window. I sensed him just inches away. Watching. Sniffing the breeze like some scent hound. Then, at last, came a clunk as the window was closed.

I didn't look back. I pushed off the wall with all my might and jumped into the dark. Something loomed in front of me. My hands went out. And . . . *smack*. I fell hard against the railings, then slid to the floor.

My hip hurt and I could taste blood. But I'd made it. I kept very still for what felt like an age. At Mr Wellbeloved's window the curtains were now drawn. Everything got darker, and I gasped in relief.

I got up slowly. My mouth was a little bloody but I wasn't badly hurt. I tapped softly at Gabriel's window. No answer. I tried to pull it open, but like mine it was locked. I pressed my ear to the glass. No sounds inside either.

'Gabriel,' I hissed. 'Let me in.'

No reply.

I tried again. Still nothing.

A little top window had been left open. Standing on tiptoe I could just reach it. I slid my arm in. My fingertips brushed the main window bolt. A twist and a heave and it opened. I slipped inside.

The room was dark and stuffy.

'Gabriel?'

My stomach dropped. There was no one here. The bed wasn't slept in. The lock on the door had been forced from the inside. Yet Gabriel's kitbag was still on the chair. His shoes were here too, placed neatly on the rug. I prayed he hadn't done a runner, that perhaps like me he just couldn't sleep.

CHAPTER 26

The gates to the pleasure gardens were locked. But by now the moon was up, and I saw the hedge was full of person-sized holes. Once I'd crawled through, I followed the path to the gorge. It was as good a place as any to look for Gabriel.

I'd only gone a few yards down it when a man stepped out in front of me. In the moonlight my nightshift glowed like a lamp. There was no point hiding.

'Where you going, ladydeee?'

Even shouting above the roar of the Falls his voice had a nasty drawl to it. I couldn't see his face, but his neck was as wide as his head.

'Just walking,' I said.

'Well, you turn round and walk that a-way,' he said, jerking his chin towards town. He was some sort of watchman, I guessed, keeping guard over I-didn't-know-what.

By chance I looked skywards. We stood right under a huge splay of guy ropes. They reached high above the trees and then went down into the earth. My mouth fell open. Tomorrow I'd be trusting these ropes with my life. Instinctively, I touched one, feeling it tight and smooth against my fingers.

Keep me safe. Keep us both safe.

'Take your hands off!' the watchman shouted. 'And get gone!'

He came towards me. I smelled whisky on his breath. I stepped backwards, as if to do as he said. Then, flash quick, I shot right round him, and ran like bleeding hell.

Very soon I reached the edge of the gorge. The path curved to run alongside it. I kept going. The Falls drowned out everything, though I sensed the watchman still behind me. At last, I risked looking round. I'd lost him. I slowed to a jog, then a walk. The path was slippery wet underfoot and mist hung heavy in the air. Still no one appeared. I stopped to draw breath.

A hand shot out of the bushes and grabbed my arm. A scream filled my throat. The hand became an arm, then a boy in a crumpled dark suit with damp hair flopping forward on his face.

I nearly choked in relief. 'Gabriel!' I gasped. 'I've been looking for you!'

'Here I am,' he said.

'What on earth are you up to?' I said, very aware that I was bare-footed and in my nightgown.

'I came to have a look,' he said. 'Have you seen it?'

'The guy ropes?'

'And the rest.' He held out his hand. 'Come with me.'

I took his hand. It was cold and trembling. Quickly, he led me the way I'd just come. I held back, trying to tell him the watchman was down here, and if he found us we'd be someone's kippers for breakfast. Gabriel didn't stop, not until we veered left off the path.

He dropped my hand. 'This is it. The starting point.'

This morning it hadn't been finished: now it was. The grass was cropped so short it felt spiky beneath my feet. Then I saw benches, rows and rows of them in lines, like I'd imagined a school might look. My heart began to race. There were more guy ropes too, and a set of wooden steps. And above us, a taut black line; the tightrope itself.

'Well I never,' I said, gazing upwards in awe.

The world seemed to fold in on itself very slowly.

No sound, no thoughts, no sense of anything else.

It was me. And the rope.

A tingling spread down my back, into my legs and toes. I saw myself walking out over the Falls, every step, every breath passing through me to the rope and back again. On and on, a continuous, magical loop.

I would not, *could not* fail.

I gazed until my neck ached. Then I said out loud, 'I can do this. I am ready.'

But looking at Gabriel, I winced. He was slumped on the steps, head in his hands.

'I can't do it, Louie,' he said. 'I know I can't.'

I went to him, taking hold of his wrists and gently pushing them aside. I wanted to see his face, and for him to see mine, so filled up with magic.

'Yes,' I said, 'you can. You did it today, didn't you?'

Our eyes locked. Then he breathed out slowly through his teeth.

'What I'd give to have your courage, Louie,' he said. 'Even a piece of it would be enough.'

Letting go of Gabriel, I took a step back. I didn't have courage for everything, not really. What I had was a way of shutting things out. Anything that hurt me or made me uncertain and – *bam* – the door closed on it. But tonight was different. I wanted to talk.

'Can I tell you something?' I said.

'If you like.'

My knees shook a little. I took a very deep breath.

'My mam left me at Chipchase's when I was a baby. I ain't seen her since, and all this time I've been angry that she didn't come back for me like she promised.'

Gabriel didn't say anything, so I kept going. 'See, I reckon I was scared. It was easier to be angry than be hurt. But you've made me think, Gabriel. And I see now that really she *did* care about me. It just might not have looked that way.'

'And Mr Chipchase?' he said.

'Yes, maybe he cared too.'

'It's been quite a day for revelations, hasn't it?'

I smiled. 'It has.'

'And your mother? Is she still alive?'

'I think so. I've a hunch she might be here in America, though I don't know where. And that maybe Mr Wellbeloved knows something.'

It sounded wild and silly, but I had to share it.

'You might be on to something,' he said. 'Mr Wellbeloved is fixated on you, Louie. Far more than he's ever been on me.'

I shuddered. 'Really?'

'Yes. The question is – why?'

I'd hoped it might be my talent for the tightrope. But Gabriel was right; there was something more.

I took another long breath.

Think of the rope, Louie.

For the tightrope was different to the way I'd felt about Mam. Or maybe, thinking of it now, it wasn't. It was about focusing on the safe part, not the dangers below. It was trusting that whatever happened, you'd get to the other side. I had courage for that. Yet how could I give some of it to Gabriel? Especially when Mr Wellbeloved had taken so much of it away.

The Falls kept rumbling. Not far off, lanterns moved through the trees. My stomach tightened; we didn't have long.

'Would you try something?' I said.

Gabriel's face fell. 'No, Louie. It won't work. I'm not really cured. You see, I do still fear the rope. I don't trust it like you do, not after what happened to Albert.'

'Climb those steps,' I said, pointing to the ones that led up to the tightrope.

Gabriel looked at me.

'Just climb them, that's all.'

He shrugged. 'All right.'

Once he'd reached the top, I took my spot on the bottom step.

He glanced over his shoulder. 'Stay there.'

'Promise,' I said, holding up my hands.

He stood very still with his back to me. I waited. If it worked, he'd find his own courage. If it didn't, he'd turn round again, and we'd have to deal with tomorrow some other way.

I watched.

After a bit, Gabriel straightened up. He flexed his feet. Next thing, he stepped out onto the rope. I gripped the handrail. *Keep going, Gabriel. Keep walking.* I counted to twenty in my head, then climbed the steps. And when I saw he'd only walked four or five strides out and was still standing above the trees, I was sorry. It hadn't worked after all. He'd frozen up again and now I'd need to talk him down.

'Step back slowly,' I yelled. 'Take your time.'

I thought he hadn't heard me. Then I gasped. Gabriel hadn't frozen, not in the slightest. He began to twirl his arms, first one way, then the other, and stretched out each leg in turn with all the grace, all the talent I knew he had in him. He took two, three, four more steps out. Now he was right above the gorge. He spun round on one foot, a great smile on his face.

I could've burst with happiness. He'd found his courage; it was there for all to see, glowing in him like fire. Anyone brave enough to walk the Falls could stand up to Mr Wellbeloved. This time, I reckoned Gabriel would, and he'd be heard.

'All right, so you *can* do it! Come on back now!' I cried, laughing and waving.

Instead, Gabriel turned again and went further out onto the rope. My arm fell to my side. It was time for me to find my courage too. Once he came down off the rope, we'd talk some more about my hunch concerning Mam.

Suddenly, the ground shook beneath my feet. I grabbed the handrail. The vibration went right up my arm. I spun round. The watchman and his mate were climbing the steps towards me.

'Now we've got her!' he leered.

I edged backwards up the steps. The watchman gritted his teeth and made a grab for me. I dodged sideways. A hand snatched my foot, but I kicked it off. I took another step back. Behind me was the tightrope with Gabriel on it. Twisting round, I tried to warn him.

He wasn't there.

'Gabriel?' I cried in alarm.

A moment ago he'd been walking the tightrope. Now all that remained was the empty rope, and the spray around it. Far below, the river surged onwards, swirling, seething white.

I screamed at the top of my lungs, 'Gabriel! *Gabriel!*'

The roar of the Falls was louder. Two sets of fingers clamped around my arms, tugging me down. I scrambled backwards as far as I could go. Then I ran out of steps.

CHAPTER 27

Mr Wellbeloved didn't take kindly to being roused from his bed.

'What the BLAZES is going on?' he cried, seeing me in the hallway with two thuggish types holding my arms.

'We caught her messing with the rigging,' said the watchman proudly.

Mr Wellbeloved glared at me. He wasn't wearing his hat, though by now I was past caring.

'Release her immediately,' he said.

The men grunted in surprise. They let go of me and I swayed on my feet.

'And the boy?' Mr Wellbeloved demanded. 'Was he with her?'

'No boy, sir. Least there was one, but he went over the edge.'

I started to cry. Mr Wellbeloved breathed out through his teeth. It made a hissing sound.

'Is there a body?'

'No, sir, no body. River tends to spew 'em up further downstream. We'll search the rapids first thing in the morning.'

I couldn't bear to listen.

'Until tomorrow then,' Mr Wellbeloved said. And he sent the men on their way.

All I wanted was to get into bed and pull the covers over my head. I tried to sneak past Mr Wellbeloved, but he dragged me by the wrist back upstairs to his room. It was hot in there and smelled of sleep. Mr Wellbeloved leaned against the door, arms folded over his chest. My palms began to sweat. I didn't like it when he blocked the way out.

'Well?' he said.

His eyes pinned me to the spot. I didn't want to keep crying, but I really couldn't stop. 'We were only on a walk,' I sobbed. 'It was too hot to sleep, and then . . .'

Mr Wellbeloved rushed at me, seizing my face.

'You silly little fool! A walk by moonlight, eh? How *preposterously* romantic.'

I tried to turn away but he held me fast.

'And now Gabriel Swift is DEAD.'

I shut my eyes.

'Look at me when I speak to you.'

I couldn't do it.

'Damn it, girl, LOOK AT ME!'

He yanked my chin towards him. As I forced my eyes open, at last I saw what his hat had been hiding.

Now I couldn't look away.

He saw my shock and panicked. His free hand went up to cover his ear. It was too late; I'd already seen it. The top half of his right ear was completely missing. What remained was mangled. The edge of it was all wavy-shaped, like a person's teeth might make.

Someone had bitten it off.

I didn't get another look. Shoving me aside, Mr Wellbeloved snatched up his hat off a nearby chair and jammed it on his head. It looked ridiculous, especially as he still wore his night clothes. A muscle hammered in his jaw. But he didn't come at me again.

'So,' he said, leaning back against the door. 'What are we to do?'

'It wouldn't be right to perform, not now Gabriel is . . .' I couldn't bring myself to say 'dead'. What I meant was that my heart wouldn't stand it. But Mr Wellbeloved looked at me like I was speaking another language.

'What, and let the ticket-buying public down?'

My face flushed hot. 'It's not fair.'

'*Fair?* What has *fair* got to do with it?'

'This isn't my doing!' And I wanted to say more, how *he'd* beaten every ounce of courage out of Gabriel Swift. *He'd* done that. Not me. But the words stuck in my throat.

Dismissively, he waved his hand. 'Say what you will. Gabriel was too flighty. We're better off without him.'

I stared at him. The man was a monster. A devil.

'Don't look so surprised. I've waited years for this.' And he indicated the wall full of photographs.

I saw them properly now. How could I not have recognised them? Picture after picture showed a man with a pointed beard. Most of them I owned myself. They were stuck inside my scrapbook.

'The Great Blondin,' I gasped.

'He had so many ways of wowing the crowds,' said Mr Wellbeloved. 'No one could better him. As a performer myself, I tried and I failed. But I never forgot him.'

He seemed almost wistful. And for a tiny, surprising moment, I understood how he felt. But I didn't understand his jealous rage at Blondin and his daughter, or how he'd put Gabriel through a living hell. I shuddered uncontrollably.

'Eventually, the crowds grew bored of him,' said Mr Wellbeloved. 'They wanted more danger. And he had none left to give. But I did, or at least my act did.'

'How?' I said, unsure I wanted to hear his answer.

His pale eyes glittered. 'Two people on the rope – you know how hard *that* is, Louisa. It was my great idea. Then Blondin copied me. *He* copied *me*, the swine. Can you believe it?'

I couldn't. Not any of it.

'Anyway, my idea proved . . .' he rubbed his jaw, '. . . *difficult* to arrange.'

'What do you mean?'

'Eventually, to fulfil my dreams I had to cast my net further afield. It took years. I thought I'd found the answer in the Swift brothers. Alas, it wasn't to be.'

I was more confused than ever. Hadn't the trick that killed Albert Swift been copied from Blondin? Or was it the other way round? It was all too much. I shut my eyes. But the horror of it didn't go away.

'So, you're my last hope, Louisa. Tomorrow I'm expecting somersaults galore. And at the end, you'll challenge a young person in the crowd to join you on the rope.'

My eyes flew open. *Was he completely mad?*

'I won't do it,' I said.

'Two people on the rope, that's the deal.'

'But . . .' I could hardly get the words out. 'The punters won't like it. They'll just leave. They won't . . .'

He seized my face again. 'You'll do it.' His tone was deadly. 'Every last bit of it. This is *my* show and you will do as I say. You won't go home to England until it's done.'

A sob broke from my mouth.

Then someone knocked at the door. 'Mr Wellbeloved, are you there?'

It was Mrs Franklin. I was ridiculously glad to hear her voice. Mr Wellbeloved rolled his eyes. 'What is it?' he said, letting go of me to open the door a sliver.

'Two gentlemen of the law are downstairs wishing to see you,' she said.

Mr Wellbeloved stepped out onto the landing. He still held the door handle, trapping me inside. From the wall, Blondin stared down at me. I couldn't bear to be here. There had to be another way out of this room.

I tiptoed across to the windows, trying each one. They were all locked. In despair, I faced the door again, thinking I'd have to barge my way out and hope Mrs Franklin might save me. It was then I caught sight of the desk.

It was still a great mess of papers; contracts, I

supposed, and letters of business. In among them was something red. It stood out like a scream. I glanced at the door. *Still shut.* With shaking fingers, I reached towards the desk.

It was a tunic. The fabric was silky smooth, of the type a performer might wear. As I held it to the lamplight, I went hot. Then cold. *It couldn't be, could it?*

The door swung open. I whisked the tunic behind my back.

'To bed,' Mr Wellbeloved ordered.

By some stroke of luck, he didn't look at me again. He simply held the door open wide for me to pass.

*

First light, I drew back the curtains. My eyes were raw from crying and I felt oddly light, like I was hollow inside. Already down by the river's edge there were men with dogs, searching for Gabriel. There was no Pip here to comfort me. No Jasper to offer kind words. I stepped back from the window, quite unable to watch.

Then I remembered the red tunic, and laid it out on my bed. There was a hole near the shoulder. Just as I'd suspected, it was shaped like a heart. I fumbled under the pillow for my scrap of red taffeta and placed it over the hole. The fit, the colour were a perfect match.

My eyes couldn't make sense of it. My brain neither. This was Mam's tunic. *My* mam's tunic. When at last my head cleared, I saw what it meant. My hunch had been right, and here was the proof. I'd found her.

Or part of her.

Could it really be true?

Mr Wellbeloved seemed to know me from times gone by. And in tracking down Gabriel, he'd found me again by chance. With a shiver, I wondered how long he'd been looking, and why.

Maybe Mr Chipchase had been expecting him *and* my mam . . . The circus's constant moving on, the clown suits, the plaited hair, they were all Mr Chipchase's way of keeping me hidden. He had his reasons for not making me showstopper; I saw that now. It had little to do with do-gooders. He'd been trying to keep me safe from danger of a very different kind. Gabriel was right: he really did care.

For quite a while I simply sat, head in hands. It was too much to take in. More than ever, I just wanted to go home.

Yet things weren't finished. I'd not come this far to

turn my back on a dream. I'd walk that rope today. And walk it like a true showstopper. Not for Mr Wellbeloved and his twisted motives, but for me, for Gabriel and for Mam.

A soft knock at the door brought me up sharp.

'Yes?'

'It's me, dear,' said Mrs Franklin. 'May I come in?'

My first thought was Gabriel: she'd come with news. As she bustled in with hot water and an armful of linen, I felt ill with dread. Setting it all down, she faced me. Something *was* wrong. She twisted her wedding ring, and opened and shut her mouth like a fish. I couldn't bear it.

'They've found Gabriel, haven't they?' I said.

She looked taken aback. 'No, dear. There's been no sign of a body.'

My legs went wobbly. I sank down on the bed. No body. No sign of him. So no proof that he'd perished. Yet.

The tiniest flicker of hope grew in me. Gabriel was a master of the tightrope. Perhaps . . . just perhaps . . .

Mrs Franklin hadn't moved.

I sighed. 'So what is it, then?'

She glanced at the door, then back at me. From her pocket she pulled out a long white envelope.

'I have some information for you. I think you'll be pleased, though what's inside will be a shock to you.'

She handed me the envelope. It was addressed to 'Mr Gideon Wellbeloved.'

'Didn't you collect this from the post office yesterday?' I said, taking it from her.

She nodded. 'Bills. Every month they send them. He never collects them himself, and he never reads them either.'

I'd no idea who 'they' were or what the bills were for. Clearly Mrs Franklin did, for she was twisting her ring again. It made me nervous.

'All these years, he's sworn me to secrecy. Said he'd make life hell for me if I told anyone.' Her voice wavered. 'But I never *liked* what he'd done. It wasn't ever right. When I realised who you were, and what he'd brought you here to do . . .'

'I don't understand,' I said. I'd not known Mrs Franklin, not until two days ago. How did she know who *I* was?

'You've your mother's fine looks,' she said. 'And I knew your first name. Goodness knows I'd heard it enough within these four walls.'

'So was she here?'

'Many years ago, yes. Then she went away. You have a right to know where she ended up.'

My mother.

All this time she'd been an image in my head. Now she was taking shape before me, and I felt overwhelmed.

I picked up the letter. *Courage, Louie.* I tore open the seal and unfolded a piece of white paper. The page was a list of dates and numbers. Some of it was written in red. At the top was a name: GOLDEN HILL RETREAT. Beneath it was a little ink drawing of a house. It looked a grand old place with tall windows and steps leading up to the door. It was all very nice. A bit *too* nice.

I gazed at those three words in a kind of stupor. Golden Hill Retreat. It sounded like the name of a hotel. An awful nice hotel. The sort of place you'd never want to leave. My hand fell to my side.

So much for promises.

Mam said she'd come back for me. Mr Chipchase was expecting her. Instead, she'd found somewhere better and not given any of us another thought.

'You're upset, dear,' said Mrs Franklin. 'It's quite a shock.'

'Am I? Is it?'

I didn't know what to think. Before I could make sense of it, the door swung open. Mr Wellbeloved strode into the room. He glanced suspiciously at Mrs Franklin, then at me. I'd hidden the piece of paper behind my back just in the nick of time.

'Let's not dally ladies,' he said. 'Louisa's to be downstairs in ten minutes.'

With a touch of his hat, he left us again.

'We'll talk more of your mother later, dear,' whispered Mrs Franklin.

I didn't answer.

I was done with talking about Mam.

CHAPTER 28

My costume, at least, was perfect: a sea-green bodice with short, puffy skirts, and tights that glittered silver. The red taffeta heart stayed in my room. No tarot cards or good luck charms could help me now. This was down to me.

The performance was scheduled for 2 p.m. First, I had to meet the press.

'I'll do the talking,' Mr Wellbeloved said.

I was glad. Already too much was jammed inside my brain; if I had to speak I didn't know what would spill out. Hand firmly on my back, Mr Wellbeloved steered me through the pleasure gardens. Everywhere I looked was a teeming mass of white frocks and best hats. There were freak shows, magic shows, performing dogs that'd put Pip to shame. The band played 'God Save the Queen', and the air, rich with burned caramel and sun-warmed grass, smelled of dreams. Not Mr Wellbeloved's, which were the stuff of nightmares, but *my* dreams. I'd come to America for this moment. It should've thrilled me, but somehow it made me feel my own misery even more.

The press were waiting in a special tent. Every morning paper had been full of me: 'CHILD TO BRAVE NIAGARA – LITTLE MISS BLONDIN BARES HER NERVES.'

There was no mention of Gabriel. It was as if he'd vanished into thin air. Which in a way he had; there one minute, nothing but mist the next. I could hardly bear to think of it. So it was a relief not to read it in the papers. I guessed Mr Wellbeloved had paid someone to keep it quiet. That would all change if a body appeared; thank heck it hadn't yet.

Inside the tent there was a scramble for seats. Mr Wellbeloved led me towards two chairs on a little stage at the front. I took the seat nearest me. Perhaps it was the gazing at a tentful of strangers, or maybe it was that damp-grass smell and the glow of canvas in the sun – whatever it was, at that moment something stirred in me. My spirits began to rise. I was a showstopper. And come what may, the show must go on.

The first reporter to stand up was a man in a brown suit. 'Charles Wheeler, *Chicago Tribune*,' he said, then to me, 'How ya feelin'?'

I smiled. *Alive.*

'She's a little nervous,' Mr Wellbeloved cut in. 'Next question.'

Two rows back, another man. 'Henry Mason, *Cleveland Morning Leader*. How long have you been in training?'

All my life.

'Long enough,' said Mr Wellbeloved. 'Louisa has a rare talent and great determination. She begged me for this chance. Next question.'

That's not the whole story, not by half.

'Robert Cleaves, *New York Daily*. Who inspires you?'

No contest. Gabriel Swift.

'Why Blondin, of course, hence the name "Little Miss Blondin". Louisa chose it herself.'

Liar. I shifted in my seat.

'Oliver Gooding, *New York Morning Herald*. Wasn't there also a boy in your act?'

Mr Wellbeloved hesitated. 'He was taken ill.'

More lies. Big, stinking lies.

'The performance will be every bit as marvellous. And at the very end there will be an extra surprise, mark my words.'

I bit my lip. *Madman.*

It went on like this for another ten minutes. The reporters had stopped writing. This wasn't the story they were after, I could tell, for they kept nodding at me, willing me to speak. So much so it gave me the bare bones of an idea. But I kept quiet all the same.

The questions were almost over, when a man said, 'Benjamin Graham, *Buffalo Post*. Rumour has it Louisa's mother was a tightrope walker. Can you confirm this?'

Bewildered, I turned to Mr Wellbeloved.

Tell them. Tell me. Is it true?

All the reporters were writing now. They'd seen my shock, there was no hiding it. Mr Wellbeloved's jaw tensed. He was rattled. So was I.

Touching his hat brim he got to his feet, dragging me with him.

'No further questions,' he said.

Yet I had a million to ask. Mr Wellbeloved knew about my mam and even if it hurt to hear it, I wanted every scrap of the truth.

He marched me fast across the park, hand clamped on my arm.

'Let go of me!' I cried.

'You took something from my room last night,

young lady,' he said, tightening his grip. 'And I want it back.'

I dug my heels into the ground.

'You took something of mine too,' I spat. 'And I want *her* back.'

He stopped dead and shook me so hard my teeth rattled. Then he marched on again, faster than ever. The crowds parted for us. Faces stared. At every step I grew more furious.

Finally, we reached the tightrope. He let me go with a shove.

'We're starting early,' he said.

This wasn't good. I needed to be calm and clear-headed to feel the magic again.

'I'm not ready,' I said.

He put his face close to mine. I recoiled.

'Remember what I want from you, Louisa.' He reached into his pocket. Pulling out a piece of paper, he mimed ripping it in two. The words 'First Class: SS *Marathon*' were obvious.

I blinked back angry tears.

Shut it out, Louie. Clear your mind.

The crowds had followed us over. People were now taking their places. There were murmurings about Gabriel's whereabouts, especially among the girls, who twisted in their seats, hoping he'd show up at the last minute. He didn't, of course. Mr Wellbeloved beckoned to his men. A few nods. A curt signal, and an announcement was made. I had seconds to compose myself.

Think only of the rope.

At the top of the wooden steps I turned and waved. Goodness, there were people EVERYWHERE. All the paid-for seats were full. Up in the trees, legs dangled off branches, faces peered through the leaves. And all along the gorge, people lined the path. The other side of the river was the same. I couldn't believe my eyes.

Focus, Louie.

I took a long breath in. And out. I shook back my hair. Straightened my shoulders. Waited for the magic to start.

Quietly now. Let it come.

I blocked out the crowd. Blocked out Mr Wellbeloved and Gabriel and Mam. Blocked out Jasper and Pip, and Chipchase's Travelling Circus. It was all too heavy to carry with me. I had to be light as air. Then, only then, would the magic work.

Let it come.

The tingling started in my feet. Like heat, it spread

273

up me until I was full. I stepped up onto the rope. Someone handed me the balance pole. Rosin coated my fingers. Behind me, a voice counted down.

'Five . . . four . . . three . . . two . . .'

A gun fired. It was my signal to start. The crowd went silent. Only the rope mattered now.

The first few steps took me out over the trees. Guy ropes led off sideways like giant ribs. I went slowly, feeling with my feet, letting the rope get used to me. The trees gave way to rocks, then water. The air grew cool. I smelled river. The roar of water made my ears sing. A few more steps and I stopped. The balance pole dipped left, then righted itself as I shifted my weight to look about me. Blondin had done it blindfolded. Not me. I wanted to see it all.

Some thousand feet up ahead was Canada. To my right was the rail bridge, crammed full of people, all peering through the bars. Everything in between was water. Below me, it churned white over the rapids. To my left, it crashed over Horseshoe Falls. In the middle of it all was a steamboat, *The Maid of the Mist*, full of spectators. Raising my arm, I waved down at them, then did the same to the shoreline and the bridge. A cheer might've gone up, but I was deaf to anything but the river.

Out in the middle, the rope began to sway; I'd expected it. Slowing again, I used my legs and the balance pole to keep steady. The mist came up fast, drenching me to the skin. The pole grew slippery. My fingers went chill and the rope seemed heavier, stickier.

Keep moving.

A few more steps and the mist cleared. Sunlight fell on my face. The rope grew still. My knees relaxed, and suddenly it felt easy again. As my strides grew longer, I even imagined myself strolling down the street with Pip at my heels, and the thought made the magic flow faster. It was like walking on air.

Up ahead, the rock face looked blindingly white. Canada was perhaps only a hundred feet away now. I saw faces again. Mouths hung open. People clutched each other in terror and excitement. A little shiver went down my back. With all eyes on me, how could I resist? It was time for some tricks. I was a showstopper, after all.

First, I sat down. Then, one leg dangling for balance, I laid out on the rope. It trembled beneath me, cutting into my shoulders and the back of my skull. Slowly, I sat up again, breathed deep, turned, and went backwards. America looked a long way away now. A few more steps and I spun round, once, twice, three times, but it sent the balance pole whirling, so I had to stop. It was enough for the look on people's faces. My heart beat wildly. I ran the last few yards.

Loud cheering and band music greeted me.

'Sixteen minutes!' a man shouted, clapping me on the back. 'Faster than Blondin himself!'

A blanket was thrown around my shoulders. My teeth chattered madly but I couldn't stop beaming. I'd done it. I really had done it.

No chance to dwell. I was rushed to a room in a smart hotel, where a lady gave me hot sweet coffee. Strangers marvelled at me. Told me I was a wonder. Dazed, I kept smiling. Then watches were consulted and my blanket and coffee cup were whisked away. It was time for Little Miss Blondin to walk home.

Going back was easier. My legs felt more used to rope-walking than to dry land. Waving farewell to Canada, I soon found my stride. The Falls were to my right now, the rail bridge to my left. A few turns, more waving, and I was back in the middle again. I slowed down.

Stay focused. Feel the rope.

I slid one foot forward. Then the other. The rope quivered. This time it didn't sway. My hair stuck to my cheeks. It was hard to see anything. All around me was white, like snow. But it didn't fool me. One wrong step and the river was waiting. I kept moving.

Four more steps and the mist lifted. Either side of me, the guy ropes appeared again. The river's edge wasn't far now. Up ahead, the crowd waited. Right at the very front was a man in a tall top hat. A few steps closer and I could make out his face. It was set with the most sickening smile. He was trying to tell me something and making a spinning action with his hands. I knew what he meant. He wanted his double somersault. It was Blondin's daughter all over again.

And I was about to say no.

I flung the balance pole into the torrent below. The crowd cried out in horror, following it all the way down with their eyes. Next, I stood on one leg. When I swapped over, I wobbled on purpose, then strode forwards with great raking steps. The river bank was so close I could smell roasting corn from the food stalls. The officials stood alongside Mr Wellbeloved now. They looked concerned. Yet still Mr Wellbeloved nodded his head at me, turning his nasty hands.

He wanted more danger?

He could have it. In fact, I hoped he'd choke on it.

Right at the last moment, I made my foot slip on purpose. My arms flew up. The crowd gasped. People started screaming. An official shouted from the bank, 'Get her back here, NOW!'

Hands reached out to me, and then I was back at the top of the wooden steps again. Despite the applause, I didn't smile. My legs had gone weak. The sun was burning hot. I felt strangely light-headed and needed to sit down.

Except I wasn't finished yet.

Mr Wellbeloved came up the steps, arms open wide.

'Well done!' he cried, though his eyes were like a snake's.

Turning from him, I faced the crowd. The size of it hit me all over again, a great sea of hats, and hands shielding faces from the afternoon sun. I raised my arm for quiet. The music trailed off. People fell silent. Mr Wellbeloved froze in his tracks.

'Do you believe I can do it all over again?' I said, for Blondin himself had asked the very same question.

'Yes!' cheered the crowd.

He'd got the same answer too. I waited for the noise to die down.

'Then who wants to come with me?'

Stunned silence.

'If you believe *I* can do it, then surely one of you can too?'

Bewildered glances. Mutterings in the crowd. Looking down, I saw Mrs Franklin press a hankie to her mouth. The reporters had their notebooks ready as Mr Wellbeloved advanced up the steps.

'Oh, look!' I cried. 'Here's my manager. Has he come to take up the challenge?'

'That would be selfish of me,' he said, speaking softly so only I could hear him. 'You must allow this young lady the pleasure.'

A child appeared from behind him. She clutched her rag doll tight to her chest. Her eyes were wet like she'd been crying.

When I could speak, I said, 'Take her back to her mother.'

'She's an orphan. No one will miss her.'

I flinched.

'Remember our deal,' Mr Wellbeloved said, trying to give me the girl's hand. 'Two people. On the rope.'

'You're mad.'

'Perhaps. But even Blondin never managed it here at Niagara. He only *carried* someone. Whereas this young child will walk with you. You see, I'll beat him yet.'

I hid my hands behind my back. 'I won't do it.'

The crowd was growing restless. Stood between us, the little girl had started crying again. I didn't know what else to do, other than carry on as if she wasn't even there.

'So, will *you* do it, Mr Wellbeloved?' I yelled for all to hear. 'Will you walk the rope with me?'

The crowd cheered.

'Don't be absurd.'

'Blondin's manager crossed Niagara on his back. Obviously, I can't carry you, but . . .'

'You've said enough.'

He'd driven Gabriel to his death. He knew something of my mam. He'd just watched me cross Niagara Falls. And still he wanted more.

He could have more.

'Mr Wellbeloved,' I said. 'I've only just got started.'

CHAPTER 29

The crowd knew something was amiss. An uneasy silence fell. With all those faces looking at me, my mouth went suddenly dry. Right now I wasn't a showstopper; I was a girl who wanted answers. And that needed a different kind of courage, the kind that faced the truth. What I did know was the power of a newspaper headline. Mr Chipchase had drummed it into me. *Louie*, he'd said, *the pen is mightier than the sword*.

The battle was about to commence.

In the very front row was the brown-suited reporter. I started with him.

'You, mister,' I called out. 'You asked earlier how I felt. Well, I'm angry. Furious and proper angry. Got that?'

The reporter raised his eyebrows. The crowd muttered in surprise. On the steps, Mr Wellbeloved stiffened.

'Why, young lady?' the reporter said. 'You've just done an amazing thing.'

'I have,' I agreed. 'But to my manager that ain't enough. He wanted a double somersault at the end. And that wasn't all . . .'

'Now just a minute,' said Mr Wellbeloved.

The little girl looked up at him, terrified. He took a step towards me, but as the crowd grew louder he stopped. I waited for quiet. My hands were sweaty damp as I clasped them tight together.

'But I said no. And that's the most amazing thing I've done today.' I paused. 'Do you know what happens to folks who say no to Mr Wellbeloved?'

People exchanged glances.

'He beats them.'

The crowd groaned.

'And he horsewhips them.'

There were boos and hisses.

'And,' I said, braver now. 'He threatens to keep them from their loved ones.'

' 'Tis cruelty!' someone called out.

The little girl sobbed. I put my arm around her shoulders.

'That's not all. If they run away he hunts them down, and scares them so much they . . .' My chin trembled. 'That's why Gabriel Swift ain't here today. He found the courage to say no too.'

A great jeer went up. The reporters started scribbling madly. Mr Wellbeloved went white with rage. But now I'd started, I wasn't going to stop.

'I was asked who inspired me. And it was Blondin, once. Then I saw him put his own daughter in a wheelbarrow and push her across the rope. The poor girl was so terrified it changed everything for me. I never felt the same about him again.'

'Shame on him!' cried the crowd.

I pointed at Mr Wellbeloved, who looked ready to murder me.

'*That* man didn't think so. He says it was his own idea, and that Blondin stole it from him.'

Another jeer went up.

Mr Wellbeloved lunged at me. 'Enough!'

I stepped back smartly. The little girl ducked between us and scarpered down the steps.

'And that child there,' I pointed after her as she disappeared into the crowd. 'Ladies and gents, *she* was your big surprise this afternoon. Mr Wellbeloved here wanted *her* to walk the rope with me.'

Everything went hushed. Then a great surge of noise rose up. Fists punched the air in anger. People were chanting one word over and over: 'No, no, no!'

It went on and on.

'No, no, no!'

When I dared look at Mr Wellbeloved, his eyes locked on mine. With one finger, he patted his jacket pocket. The tip of the boat ticket poked out of it.

I gritted my teeth. 'And about my training.' Now I had to shout over the noise. 'Mr Wellbeloved didn't quite lie, because I have trained hard and I do have a talent. But there's a part he didn't tell you.'

The noise fell away. I clasped my hands to stop them trembling. This was the hardest part of all. My pulse beat so fast it made my throat go tight. I wasn't sure I could even speak.

Courage, Louie.

I breathed slowly.

'Walking the tightrope is in my blood. And as I found out today, there's word that my own mother performed the high wire herself.'

More gasps from the crowd. The reporters' heads were down, covering page after page with writing.

'I don't know the whole truth of it. But I do know she was here once, and it seems she might still be nearby.'

Someone called out, 'Is she here today?'

It didn't occur to me that she would be. But it went through the crowd like fire through a hayrick, everyone suddenly turning and pointing. Mr Wellbeloved stood silent, shaking his head.

You know exactly where she is, you devil, I thought.

In the crowd, shoulders started shrugging. People shook their heads. Seeing their faces, I felt myself go red.

Fancy her own mother not coming to see her, those looks seemed to say. Eventually, a reporter confirmed it. 'No, it seems she isn't here.'

And they wrote that down too.

A wave of tiredness hit me then. My legs swayed.

'Let the girl go,' said an official. 'She looks ready to faint.'

As I took my weary bows, the crowd clapped for a good five minutes. It was sweet music to my ears. Yet my heart seemed to lag behind. This still wasn't finished, even now.

For starters, Mr Wellbeloved still blocked the steps. The only other way out was the tightrope behind me. For a split second, I was torn: Gabriel's way out, or face Mr Wellbeloved?

I straightened my shoulders and stepped forward.

285

'Excuse me,' I said.

He didn't move. Behind him, I sensed the crowd bristling. It made me braver.

'I'd like to pass,' I said.

He still didn't shift. I stared at his chest, all tailored in a fine, striped coat with that boat ticket sticking out of his pocket. It made me think of gates on board ship, of locked doors and windows. I'd got through them all eventually. I'd kept following the trail of crumbs. Yet Mr Wellbeloved himself once said that sometimes you had to wait for a gate to open.

So I folded my arms. And waited. The crowd jeered. They didn't stop until he stepped aside.

*

Mrs Franklin took me away in a carriage. Back at the lodgings, she made me hot chocolate, then ordered me to bed. I was glad of her just in case Mr Wellbeloved returned. But news soon reached us that he'd taken the first train out of town.

'A wise move,' said Mrs Franklin, as she sat beside my bed. 'Those evening papers won't paint a pretty picture of him.'

Lying back against the pillows, I felt truly

exhausted. And oh so glad I'd never have to face Mr Wellbeloved again, except he'd vanished without paying me a single penny. I'd done a very brave thing today. Yet what did that matter if I didn't have a ticket home? Suddenly, I felt overcome.

'What is it?' said Mrs Franklin as I sobbed.

'I just want to go home. But I can't.'

'Aha! Yes you can.'

'How? I can't even pay my passage.'

She patted my hand. 'A hat was passed round today and people gave kindly, don't you fret. There's money enough to get you home.'

'Oh my word!'

Mrs Franklin pushed the damp hair off my face. 'You need your mother first though, don't you dear?'

Which set me off crying even harder.

'But she's in her nice hotel. She won't want to see me.'

The tears kept coming till my throat ached. When at last I stopped and wiped my face, Mrs Franklin was staring at me strangely.

'Hotel?' she said. 'What do you mean, *hotel*?'

'That Golden Hill place.'

Mrs Franklin took my hand. She looked very grave

indeed. 'Louie, Golden Hill Retreat isn't a hotel. Mr Wellbeloved sent your mother there when she, well, she . . . attacked him.'

I stared at her. *Attacked him?*

Mrs Franklin nodded, eyes shut.

'What did she do to him?'

It couldn't be that bad surely, not half as bad as what he did to other people. Yet, eyes open again, Mrs Franklin looked decidedly queasy.

'She bit off his ear, here in this room. And then spat it out into the fireplace.'

'That's hideous!'

I didn't know whether to laugh or heave up. It was so . . . *shocking*. No wonder Mr Wellbeloved kept his hat on, especially in front of me. A million thoughts all charged my head at once.

My mam was violent.

My mam was brave.

And yet to bite a man's ear off . . .

'Why did she do it?' I asked.

'She had her reasons,' said Mrs Franklin. 'You'll need to hear the truth from her.'

'So, should I go to her?' The idea made me nervous.

'Yes, dear.'

'Can't we invite her here to tea instead?'

She shook her head sadly. 'My dear, Golden Hill Retreat is a hospital,' she paused, 'for the *temperamentally* unwell. Mr Wellbeloved had her locked away. Your mother couldn't leave if she tried.'

CHAPTER 30

For a place named Golden Hill it was surprisingly flat and green. The road followed the shores of a lake so vast it might've been the sea. It made me ache to be on board ship, heading home. Tomorrow I would be. *We* would be. I hadn't a clue how I'd manage it, but I had no intention of leaving Mam behind.

Set back from the lake was a red brick house with a roof like a church spire. The driver dropped me at the gates.

'This is it,' he said.

Suddenly, I was gripped by nerves. The sign on the gatepost said 'Golden Hill Retreat'. There was a bell to ring for the gates to be opened.

The driver nudged me. 'Off you go. And don't forget this.'

He handed me my parcel. Tucking it under my arm, I climbed down from the carriage and pulled the bell. Inside my chest a boom-booming started, though for quite a while no one came. Finally, a woman in a grey dress and pinny appeared.

'Yes?' She made no move to open the gates.

'I've come to see my mam,' I said.

Her eyes flicked over me. 'Your mother's name?'

'Um . . .' All I knew were her initials. 'M.S. I don't know her full name.'

The woman looked blank. 'What makes you think she's with us?'

'Mr Gideon Wellbeloved sent her here. I saw the bills.'

'The bills, eh?'

I'd got her interest now.

'You've come from England. I can tell from your accent,' she said. 'And M.S. stands for Maria Samparini.'

What a name. It sounded like music.

'But there's no visiting today. You'll have to come back tomorrow.'

Tomorrow?

She might as well have tied a brick to my heart and thrown it in the lake.

'But I'm leaving for England tomorrow. You must let me see her. Please!' I cried.

The woman drummed her fingers on the gate.

'Mr Wellbeloved has received the bills, you say?'

'Yes, but I heard he never reads them,' I said, knowing from bitter experience he wasn't a good payer. But I didn't see what this had to do with Mam.

Yet it worked. With a mighty clunk, the woman opened the gates. We hurried down a driveway to the front of the house. It didn't look so swanky in real life. The gardens were all lawns and trees, with no flowers to speak of. We went up the front steps and into a dim hallway. After the bright sunlight, I saw sparkles before my eyes.

'Wait here.' The woman disappeared through a door.

Once, this might've been a smart house. There were still coloured tiles on the floor and swirls on the ceiling. The staircase curved upwards; I imagined fine ladies walking down it in their ball gowns. Now there were faded patches on the walls where pictures had once been. It was a sad sort of place to be ill in. The sooner I got Mam home, the better.

The woman reappeared with a key.

'My name is Miss Winters.'

'I'm Louie,' I said, holding out my hand.

She didn't take it.

'This is highly irregular,' she said, glancing over her shoulder. 'Follow me.'

My belly churned as I followed her up the stairs. At the very top we went down a corridor full of doorways. Miss Winters's boots tap-tapped on the bare boards. There was no other sound. The air was hot and stuffy and smelled of old dinners. Sweat prickled my neck.

Miss Winters stopped at the final door. She knocked on it lightly with her knuckles.

'Maria?' she called. 'A visitor is here to see you.'

Nervously, I shifted my parcel from one arm to the other; I wished I'd brought flowers instead. Miss Winters put her key in the lock and leaned her shoulder against the door. It opened a fraction. She looked inside, nodded, then opened it wider.

'In you go,' she said, stepping aside for me. 'Try not to excite her.'

She locked the door behind her.

The room was small with a sloping roof. A low window with bars on it looked out towards the lake. The only furniture was a bed and a chair. There was no one here. There'd been some mistake. I went to call Miss Winters, then I saw someone sitting on the floor. She had her back against the wall, her legs stretched out in front of her. Her face was turned towards the window.

My knees started shaking. In my mind's eye I'd had a picture of my mam: red hair, pale skin, easy smile. This woman wore an ugly brown frock. Her wrists and ankles stuck out of it like bird bones. Her hair wasn't bright and flowing. It was streaked with grey and plaited tight to her head. She didn't look much of a biter either. I'd seen more life in a line of laundry.

The woman sensed me watching. Slowly, she turned her head. My hands were shaking now. The parcel slipped from my grasp to the floor.

For a very long moment, the woman stared at me without blinking.

Then she frowned. 'Louie?'

The eyes looking back at me were as green as a cat's. They might've been my own.

'Yes, Mam. It's me.'

I took a few steps towards her, then stopped. Was I meant to hug her? Kiss her? I'd no idea. My feet wouldn't move. The space between us felt huge.

Then Mam reached out to me, and I joined her at the window. She touched my cheek, my hair, my shoulder, like she was checking I was real. And as she cupped my face in her hands I put my own fingers over hers just to keep them there. When she did let go it was only to hold me closer.

'My dearest girl,' she said.

We sat together on the floor in a little patch of sunlight. Tears were shed, but they were mostly happy tears. It was Mam who moved first. Stiffly, she got to her feet and made me get up too. It was only then that I truly saw how thin she was, and how I was almost as tall as her.

'Let's sit here,' she said, patting the narrow bed.

As we squeezed up together I felt her hip bone dig into mine. She smelled strongly of carbolic soap.

'How did you find me?' she said.

I didn't know where to start. With the red taffeta heart? The letter? Mr Wellbeloved's bills? As Miss Winters had said not to excite her, I wasn't sure quite *what* to say.

'Well,' I said, 'I'm with a circus.'

She smiled wearily. 'Dear Leo.'

Straight away I was thrown. 'So you *do* know Mr Chipchase?'

She shrugged. *Was that a flush on her cheeks?* My mind started racing. *Her . . . and . . . Mr Chipchase?*

It was easier to keep talking.

'I came here to perform, though not with Mr

Chipchase. But I knew from your letter you might be overseas somewhere. You see, I walk the tightrope.'

Mam rubbed her forehead. 'Slow down a little.'

She looked like she'd just woken from a dream and was still dazed by it. I slipped my fingers into hers.

'So, I walk the tightrope,' I said. 'It's my passion, and I trust it more than anything.'

A flicker came into her eyes. 'I understand,' she said.

Yet I felt her drift away from me again. She gazed into space for a very long moment. Then she spotted my parcel on the floor. 'What's this? Is it yours?'

'Actually, it's yours.'

I'd brought it here in case she hadn't recognised me. Such a thought seemed ridiculous now.

'Shall we open it?' she said.

I felt a little uneasy, not sure what she'd make of that red tunic with the heart cut out of it. But by rights it was hers; I could hardly say no. So I stood and picked up the parcel from the floor. As I undid its strings and pulled out the tunic, Mam shrank back in horror.

'Where did you get it?' she cried.

I hesitated. Again, I didn't know quite where to start – Mr Wellbeloved and his trail of crumbs, or why he still had something of hers? I hardly understood it myself.

'All these years he kept it,' she whispered. 'All these years . . .' She put her head back against the wall and closed her eyes. The pulse in her neck beat fast.

'Mam,' I said, perching on the edge of the bed beside her, 'it's all right.'

Though it was clear things weren't right at all.

CHAPTER 31

No one got well with bars on their windows. Anyone in the circus knew what it did to wild animals – it was why Mr Chipchase only kept horses. So heck knows what this locked room had done to Mam. I had to get her away from here. And fast. Even with the red tunic safely out of sight, she was still trembling hard.

'Oh no,' she said in a low moaning voice. 'Oh dear God, no.'

'What is it?'

She snatched both my hands. Right now she looked every inch the biter.

'You're here with *him*, aren't you? He hasn't hurt you, has he? Tell me he hasn't!'

I tried to pull my hands free, but she held them tight. Her fingers were burning hot. Glancing at the door, I wondered where Miss Winters was. She'd surely be due back by now.

Mam saw my alarm and loosened her grip.

'Louie, I'm sorry.' Her voice shook. 'But if you knew what evil there is in that man you'd never have come to America with him.'

I felt very uneasy. Because I did know how evil Mr Wellbeloved was, and now so did most of New York State, thanks to the papers.

'I'm not with him anymore,' I said.

'You promise me?'

'Absolutely.'

She lay back on the bed. It took a while for her trembling to ease. When it did, she shifted onto her side and gazed at me. Her nose was pink from crying.

'Many years ago I worked for Mr Chipchase. Things became ... well ... complicated.'

I didn't quite follow, but she kept talking.

'Stupidly, I wanted bigger and better things. So I left Chipchase's and joined up with . . .' she couldn't speak his name, '. . . *him*. You were not long born, and the work was hard.'

A sick thought rushed into my head. 'Mr Wellbeloved's not my . . . ?'

'No, Louie. He's not your father.'

I breathed again.

'So,' Mam continued, 'with you to care for, I had to keep working, even though it was tough, tougher than

I'd ever known at Chipchase's. No one dared cross the gaffer.'

I winced, picturing Gabriel's horsewhipped arms.

'Then he had notions about Niagara,' said Mam. 'I was dazzled by it. I was a showstopper. It was in my blood. I was also under contract to him, so I had to agree. But,' she blinked slowly, 'there was a catch.'

I shuddered. It was bound to be awful.

'He wanted me to walk the Falls with you strapped to my back . . . you were but four months old.'

It was. Truly awful.

'*Blondin*,' I said, feeling ill. 'Mr Wellbeloved said he needed a trick to outshine Blondin.'

Mam nodded. 'He was obsessed by it. But I'd have died rather than put you in that much danger. I'd never want you to cross the Falls.'

'Oh.'

I turned away. What should I tell her? That it was too late, that I *had* crossed the Falls just yesterday? That Mr Wellbeloved had set the whole thing up, and that he'd wanted me to walk the Falls all along?

It hit me *slap bang* in the face.

This wasn't about glory.

This was revenge.

Mr Wellbeloved had done this to punish Mam, all

because she'd dared to say no. On the face of it, it seemed far-fetched. Only someone truly twisted would think up such a plan. And then wait . . . and wait . . . for thirteen whole years, with all that bitterness still festering away inside them.

Mr Wellbeloved *was* that twisted. And he was persistent. A bit of luck and he'd found me through Gabriel. The rest was pure cunning: not choosing me, then welcoming me on the ship, taking the red heart and then giving it back again, even hounding Gabriel to his death. It was all part of the trail of crumbs. And it all led to one thing.

Me crossing Niagara Falls.

The realisation made it hard to breathe. I fought the urge to scream by digging my nails into my palms.

How could he, how could he, how could he?

Mam eased my hands apart. 'Louie?'

Bewildered, I looked into her eyes. They were huge and dark and stormy. But there was also a flicker of fire in them.

That fire was in me too. For I hadn't been exactly helpless in all this. I wasn't a baby strapped to its mother's back. I also had my own reasons for being here. *I'd* wanted to cross Niagara more than anything. *I'd* chosen it. And I'd done it in style. The whole world might now know of Little Miss Blondin. Yet what mattered more were the other headlines, the ones that shamed Mr Wellbeloved. That had been my work too.

'He didn't hurt you, Louie, and that's all I care about,' said Mam.

She was right. Though it didn't wipe out Mr Wellbeloved's intentions. The thought of Gabriel still made my chest hurt. I'd never forget him or his poor brother.

'So, how did you get out of performing?' I asked, wanting to hear her story much more than dwelling on mine. 'Did Mr Wellbeloved follow you? Did he whip you?'

Mam took a big, shivery breath. 'I left you behind in England. It nearly killed me to do it, but the alternative was far worse.'

'But why Chipchase's? And why Jasper's wagon? Why not a foundling hospital or an orphanage?'

Her face went soft.

Oh blimey, I thought, picturing waistcoats and angry voices, and worse, Kitty Chipchase's sour face. This time *my* cheeks flushed. *Mam and Mr Chipchase? Really?* I hardly dared think it, but I knew what it meant. Only I wasn't ready to hear it, not yet.

Mam gave my hand a little squeeze. 'That wagon,

my sweet child, was once my wagon. It was where you were born.'

I gulped. 'Was it?'

'It was. I'd heard Jasper, who'd replaced me as showstopper, was a dear man. And I wanted you to still have your home.'

Jasper replaced *Mam*?

I couldn't quite grasp it. Any of it. Yet when I pictured our wagon with its tiny bunks and cluttered shelves, the ache in my chest grew strong. It was home, and had always been home. Now I was beginning to see why.

'Chipchase's is a good circus with good people,' said Mam. 'It was the best place I knew.'

There was still so much I didn't understand. But I realised one thing for certain, even more than when I'd first read her letter. Mam hadn't left me behind like an umbrella at all. She'd left me so I'd be safe, and Chipchase's had done its very best for her. And for me.

Though her face was wet with tears now, Mam kept on with her story. 'I didn't tell that monster I'd left you behind till we'd arrived in America. All the way, I'd pretended you were sleeping in the cabin.'

'And then?'

'When I did tell him, he . . . well, there was quite a

scene. He insisted we send for you at once. I refused. Point blank.'

I shivered.

'So,' she wiped her cheek, 'he threatened to send me here. He said I'd never see you again if he did. It made me so mad I attacked him.'

'You fell into his trap, just like I did.'

'Sorry?'

At that moment the door opened. Miss Winters held it wide as a man stepped inside. Mam rose from the bed.

'What is it, Dr Grogan?' She squared her shoulders and folded her arms. Maybe I imagined it, but she looked taller too. Just like Miss Lilly's last card – the one about female power – and it made me feel brave too. Here was my mam, the empress.

The doctor took his glasses off, cleaned them, then put them back on again. He squinted like a mole.

'Ah, Miss Samparini,' he said. 'There seems to be a problem.'

Now I stood up too. Today wasn't for visitors and he'd come to ask me to leave, hadn't he? Perhaps never to come back again. A wave of panic hit me. For now I'd found Mam I couldn't bear to leave her, not even for a day. Yet I'd still not the faintest idea how to get her out of here, not without doctors or lawyers or whatever it took.

'It has come to my attention that there are six months at least of unpaid accounts,' Dr Grogan said. 'We have requested payment, but Mr Wellbeloved hasn't responded.'

'I see,' said Mam.

So did I. For hadn't there been six envelopes in Mrs Franklin's basket? That surely meant one for each unpaid month. And Mr Wellbeloved hadn't opened any of them.

'You won't find him, sir,' I said. 'Read today's papers and you'll see. He's been run out of town.'

Dr Grogan spread his hands. 'Then there is no easy way to say this, Miss Samparini. Without payment, we cannot continue to treat you.'

It took a moment to realise what he was saying. Mam turned to me, bewildered as I started to laugh. For it really was absurd. Mr Wellbeloved had never been a good payer. Gabriel had known it and so did I. He was so busy scheming he'd forgotten to pay the very bills that kept Mam from me. Odd though it was, I felt grateful. So grateful I seized Mam's hands.

'In which case,' I said, 'we're going home.'

✴ CURTAIN CALL ✴

CHAPTER 32

Fresh off the boat, we tracked down Chipchase's Travelling Circus, Mam and me. And just like he'd done all those years ago, Mr Chipchase took us in.

'So you came back, Maria,' he'd said on seeing Mam, still pale and thin but getting stronger every day. 'And aren't you a sight for sore eyes?'

For me, he had just three words, 'Well, well, well.' The look of joy on his face said the rest.

Within hours he'd made me the showstopper again. The posters went up all over town. 'BIGGEST SHOW OF THE SEASON' they said in bold blue letters. Written bigger still was 'MISS NIAGARA: THE GIRL WHO WALKS ON AIR,' the show name I'd chosen myself because that's how crossing Niagara had felt. Everyone agreed it was perfect because it told the world what I'd done. And it meant Blondin had his name back too.

Secretly, I'd thought of other names, like 'Miss

Found Her Mam' and 'Miss Said No To Mr Wellbeloved', though they didn't quite have the same ring. Nor did 'Miss Still Hurting Over Gabriel', because that was just plain miserable, even if it did happen to be true.

It was also true that Mr Chipchase was my pa, and hiding from it wouldn't change things. What surprised me was how quickly I got used to the idea. Yet I didn't want to swap the surname that had been another layer of disguise. Far safer to have been raised Reynolds than Chipchase, I saw that now.

What was in a name, anyhow? Chipchase's Travelling Circus was family to me. Had been and always would be. Though Mr Chipchase shouted and Kitty got up my nose, perhaps everyone's relatives were a tiny bit like that. And as for his fixation on Wellbeloved's Circus, I understood it now for what it had been: not an eye on the competition, but fear. Fear that a man in a too-tall hat would lure me away before my mam could reach me.

*

Now it was almost show time. Dusk was falling and dew lay thick on the grass. The tickets were all sold, the showground was filling up, and four of us were squeezed inside Paolo and Marco's wagon. This time it wasn't me fixing costumes; now I was the one being pinned and tucked. Mam and Jasper sat on the only chairs. I was better standing, for I couldn't keep my jiggling knees still. It made things hard for poor Paolo, who was trying to put the finishing touches to my tunic.

Mam narrowed her eyes. 'Make it shorter.'

Jasper disagreed. 'It needs more sparkle.'

'Enough!' I cried. 'Listen to yourselves!'

They'd argued over everything at first, right down to how I liked my lapsang tea. It felt odd having two people fighting for my affections. But things were getting better. Mam saw how I loved Jasper, and Jasper had always wanted me to know my mam.

'What do you think, Pip?' I said to my little dog, who was curled at my feet.

The tip of his tail twitched.

'Pip thinks it's fine.'

Yet I couldn't resist a glance in Paolo's mirror. And when I saw my reflection, my mouth fell open.

'Oh . . . my . . . word.'

The red taffeta tunic shimmered in the lamplight. He'd done a stunning job at repairing it, and it quite took my breath away. On the left-hand side, where a hole had once been, there was now just the faintest heart-shaped seam. Only those who knew of it would see anything amiss.

'It's wonderful,' I said, fearing I might sob.

Jasper and Mam nodded in agreement. They both had tears in their eyes.

A knock at the wagon door brought us up sharp. It was Ned, all smart in his ringmaster's hat and tails.

'Fifteen minutes to go, Louie,' he said, and then looked me over, but not in a moony way, for things were different now. 'You ready?'

'I am.'

I gave Pip a fussing, then reached for Jasper's hand. 'For luck,' I said, kissing his palm three times.

He closed his fist to keep them safe. Last of all, I hugged my mam tight.

Outside, the air smelled of autumn. Gooseflesh rose up on my arms, though it was more from excitement than the cold. We cut through the crowds, past the stalls selling toffee apples and spiced buns, which were all lit up a treat.

'She's meant to be quite something, this Miss Niagara,' I heard a punter say.

'Better than Blondin, so I've heard,' said another.

Grinning, I nudged Ned.

'That's what everyone's saying,' he said, nudging me back.

'I'm not better, just different,' I said.

Really, I'd much to thank Blondin for. His brilliance had filled my head with magic. And his mistakes had shown me a line it wasn't right to cross.

At the end of the stalls, next to the coconut shy, was Miss Lilly's tent, its coloured lights twinkling in the dusk. She was standing outside.

'Evening to you, Miss Lilly,' I said with a wave.

She dipped her head. ' 'Tis a fine night tonight, Louie.'

I was glad to hear it.

'The cards were right,' she said. 'And so were you.'

'I'll catch you up,' I said to Ned.

Turning to Miss Lilly, I felt her strangeness pull at me.

'You reached out to your mother. You faced your past.' Her voice was low and thrilling. 'Yet what of your future? It's time to reach for that also.'

'Death?' I said, for I remembered the skeleton card well.

'New beginnings, Louie, that's what the card means.

But I feel you are still fearful of something. Part of you is hiding away.'

I didn't quite follow. Hundreds of people had come to see me tonight. Here I was in short skirts, hair loose to my waist and a big smile to match. I was hardly hiding away.

Then Ned was back, tugging at my arm. 'Five minutes to go,' he said. 'Get a shift on.'

We went straight to the practice area at the back of the big top. A bonfire blazed in the middle of the makeshift ring. It cast a glow over the performers and sent twirling sparks dancing into the air. I breathed in the smell of smoke and horses, of greasepaint and earth and sheer hard work. My heart swelled. No, I didn't quite believe Miss Lilly. This was my world. And there was nothing in it to be scared of.

As I began to do my stretches, the magic took hold. Warmth spread from my toes to my fingertips, up and up to the very ends of my hair. Yet Miss Lilly's words didn't want to shift. They lodged in my head just when I needed a clear mind.

Focus, Louie.

More stretches, more breathing. Bit by bit the words went quiet.

And then other thoughts rose up in their place.

Never mind that Ned was friends with Kitty, because I was trying to be too. Perhaps all along she'd known who I was, and that doing her sums, she'd realised I was only two years younger than her, which meant her pa hadn't grieved her dead mam for long. Or it might not have been that at all. It might've been because she'd had a soft spot for Ned. And if it was, then things had a way of working themselves out. For now, just feet away from me, he had his arm around her shoulders and was grinning at her in a way he'd once grinned at me.

Keep focused. Let the magic work.

I shut my eyes.

When I opened them again, something had happened. Marco's mouth was hanging open. Rosa had slid down off her horse. And Ned, no longer mooning over Kitty, was shaking someone's hand and pointing in my direction.

A boy stepped forward. The fire lit him from behind, and although he was in shadow his outline seemed to glow. He had a kitbag slung over his shoulder and was wearing a crumpled suit. I was sure I was dreaming. Yet now the boy was nearer, there was no mistaking that floppy blond hair, or the way his chin went sharp when he smiled. No mistaking either the frantic fluttering inside me.

'Gabriel!' I breathed.

I stared at him in a kind of daze. As time had passed and no body was reported, I'd sometimes dared to hope: *perhaps he'd reached Canada. Perhaps he'd be all right.* But more often than not, all I pictured was that empty tightrope and the mist swirling around it.

'You made it,' I said.

'I did,' he said, looking almost shy.

I wondered if I should hug him. Trouble was, I was stuck to the spot.

'What . . . I mean . . . *how*?' I stammered.

'I got to Canada,' he said, 'and worked until I could pay my passage home. Then I came back to Mrs Franklin's to find you, but she said you'd gone.'

I kept staring. It was a while before I trusted myself to speak again.

'So you did it. You walked the Falls. Oh Gabriel!'

'You did too,' he smiled, '*and* you found your mother, so I hear.'

'And not before time,' I said. 'Mr Wellbeloved had got his claws into her too. What he did was shocking, even by his standards.'

'I'm so sorry,' Gabriel said. 'But you stood up to him, Louie. I read it in the papers – you shamed him out of town.'

I felt my cheeks flush. 'I think we did it together, really.'

'Did you know he tried to open another circus under a different name?'

'What, here? In England?'

Gabriel nodded. 'He changed his name to Mr Diablo.'

'That's fitting,' I said, for diablo meant the devil. 'Suits him much better than Wellbeloved.'

Gabriel looked at me and smiled. My stomach did an odd sort of swoop.

'The Society for Moral Obedience discovered how he'd treated people in his circuses,' he said, 'and they shut him down before he had the chance to open.'

'Do-gooders, eh? Who'd have thought it? Maybe they do *some* good after all.'

'Actually, what they did was say no to him.'

Agreed, it was the sweetest revenge.

The rest of the performers had gone inside the tent, for the show was starting now. Mighty Ned's voice echoed out over the showground as he welcomed tonight's crowd.

'Ladies and gentlemen . . . this is our finest show of the season . . .'

I squeezed Gabriel's hand. 'I'd better go.'

'I wanted to see you again, Louie, to know you were all right.' He kept hold of my fingers.

My insides leaped like they did when our wagon went too fast over a bridge. I couldn't seem to speak.

Eventually, he let go of me. 'Well, I suppose this is goodbye.'

'Wait!' I cried, all in a rush. 'Please! Oh do watch the show. And then . . .'

'Yes?'

'And then perhaps we could speak to Mr Chipchase about you staying on with us . . . or something . . .'

'You're his showstopper now, Louie. He doesn't need me as well.'

I reached for his hand again.

'But I do.'

Gabriel smiled. Not his normal, pleasant, mouth-curving one, but a great beam that made his whole face shine.

'Thank goodness, Louie,' he said, taking both my hands in his. 'Thank goodness.'

*

The big top was packed to the rafters. There was no rustling of papers, no clearing of throats. The silence was sharp as a blade. As I stood under the spotlight, every little part of me felt alive.

'Now . . .' cried Mighty Ned, '. . . the very moment you've been waiting for . . . where skill triumphs over weakness . . . where bravery triumphs over fear . . .'

The light was just enough to see the front row.

'Fix on a face in the crowd,' Jasper once said. 'Perform just for them.'

And tonight here he was, looking handsome as ever. To his left was Mam; she blew me a little kiss. Next to her sat Mr Chipchase, in a new tweed waistcoat. For once, the colours were quite tame. And next to him was my half-sister, Kitty, who actually looked rather pretty when she didn't scowl. Sat at the end was a boy with golden hair and a smile that could melt icebergs. On his knee, looking blissful, was my little white dog.

It was a most glorious sight. I felt fit to burst.

Yet how could I choose? It was impossible. These faces were all dear to me, every single one.

So I chose them all.

Turning from the crowds, I made my way to the ladder. I climbed it slowly, waving and smiling at every second rung. At the top, I paused. I rolled my shoulders one last time, shook out my hands, my feet. Below me, Mighty Ned talked on.

'Ladies and gentlemen . . . with great pleasure and pride . . . I give you . . . Miss Niagara: The Girl Who Walks On Air!'

Yet tonight the lightness didn't just come from my feet. It came from deep inside me, where I'd kept it hidden for far too long. And now I'd opened up at last, I was truly walking on air.

Focus, Louie.

Shutting my eyes, I waited for my head to clear. I filled my lungs. Breathed out good and slow. Nothing else mattered as I stepped out onto the tightrope. Once a showstopper, always a showstopper.

And right now, it was show time.

ACKNOWLEDGEMENTS

I'd like to say a massive thank you to the people who helped make Louie a showstopper. To my agent Jodie Hodges, who read early drafts, said 'MORE DRAMA!' then took me for afternoon tea. To all at Faber who've supported me as a writer, but in particular to my editor Rebecca Lee, whose wisdom and kind words have been invaluable. And to James Rose and Anna Swan for their copy-editing skills. Also to my publicist Hannah Love, who persuaded me to leave Somerset now and again. And to Julian de Narvaez for designing such a beautiful cover and using my dog Bagel as the model.

Thank you to the bloggers, reviewers, booksellers and librarians, who allow books to find readers. And to my writing pals on Twitter and at Author Allsorts who've offered encouragement and advice.

None of this would be possible without the love and support of friends and family. To my besties Becky Howat and Karl Watson – just because. To the

Carrolls for great dinners and bubbly. Also to my parents for putting up with the moaning – sorry about that. It can't be easy living with a writer, which is why my biggest thanks of all goes to Owen, who deserves a medal.

AN INTERVIEW WITH EMMA CARROLL

How long did it take you to write The Girl Who Walked on Air?

The first draft took ten very strict bum-on-seat months. I'm not the fastest writer by nature, so I had to be disciplined, which meant less Twitter, more writing.

How did you come up with Louie as a character?

One foggy night, Louie is found abandoned. That's how it happens in the story, and actually creating her was quite similar. She just appeared out of my brain fog.

What gave you the idea to set your book in a Victorian circus?

Once I started reading about circuses, I just *had* to write about one. The Victorians had strong stomachs for danger. Unlike nowadays, acrobats performed without safety harnesses. The fact they might fall – and many did – added to the 'sensation' of the show. For a writer, nineteenth-century female characters can be tricky. The rich ones tended to live quite restricted lives. Circuses, though, were viewed as 'outside' of respectable society, which gave Louie and me more freedom; a circus girl would travel, work, face hardships. She'd also encounter more danger – all are great story ingredients!

Can you do any circus tricks?

Not yet. But I've got double-jointed elbows that bend backwards, and I do a great imitation of a squeaky toy.

Louie goes to Niagara Falls and the descriptions are so vivid – have you been there? How do you write about a real place where you've never been?

I confess I haven't been to Niagara Falls. When I spoke to people who had, they mentioned the noise. Apparently, you can hear the Falls all over town. I also read books, pored over pictures, looked on Google Earth, watched films. It's an awesome place – no wonder so many daredevils performed there (with mixed results).

How much of the story is true?

It's true that Charles Blondin was the first person to walk Niagara Falls on 30 June 1859. Many tightrope walkers were inspired by him. It's also true that he toured the UK, performing at the Crystal Palace in 1861, with his young daughter, Adele, in a wheelbarrow. The audience were horrified and Blondin was made to vow never to attempt the trick again. The SS *Marathon* did actually exist, as did Maria Spelterini, who was the first woman to cross Niagara on 8 July 1876. Over a two-week period, she repeated the feat many times, then mysteriously disappeared. Louie's mother is based on her. It's also true that 'do-gooders' put pressure on circuses not to use child performers. In 1879 the Dangerous Performances Act banned performers under the age of fourteen. My story is set just before that time.

Louie has a pet dog, Pip. Did you have any pets growing up?

We had a bonkers Boxer dog called Kizzy. She was always up for a bit of mischief, which is just how a dog should be. We were inseparable.

Which character are you most like?

Probably Gabriel. I can't imagine how anyone would trust a tightrope!

When did you know you wanted to be an author?

I got the story-writing bug at a very early age, though I had a big gap of about twenty years where I didn't write anything. Yet I'd daydream about being a writer one day. Finally, it's happened. I still have to pinch myself!

What's a typical working day like for an author?

First of all, I drink tea and read. Then I walk my dogs. After that, I'll settle down to write, usually by about 10 a.m. I make notes and do rough plans in notebooks, but write straight on to my laptop. On a first draft, I'll aim for a minimum of a thousand words a day. There are other parts to being a writer, too, like answering emails, doing edits, promo work, writing blogs, etc. And Twitter, which does count, doesn't it?

When you have finished writing a book, who is your first reader?

With *Frost Hollow Hall* it was my closest friends and

family because I didn't have a book deal then. This time round it's been my agent and my editor. Everyone else will get to read it when it's a lovely printed book, which is far nicer than squinting at a computer screen.

Are you influenced by any other authors?

Absolutely. I read constantly. A successful children's writer once described reading as 'nourishment', which I think sums it up nicely.

Which were your favourite books when you were a child?

All the Moomin stories. Anything with a horse in it – I had shelves and shelves of pony books. My absolute favourites were the Jinny at Finmory series by Patricia Leitch. A few years ago, I bought them again off Ebay. They're still wonderful stories.

What ingredients does a good book need?

Three-dimensional characters, strong settings, plot twists – a bit of snow doesn't hurt either.

Do you have any tips for new writers?

Hmm . . . I still feel like a new writer myself, so I'd say

practise lots. You won't always get it right, but that's part of the process.

What do you like to do besides write?

Read. Walk my dogs. Hang out with friends and family. Go shopping with my mum. Eat – I'm lucky that my husband is a brilliant cook.

Are you able to tell us anything about your next book?

It's about woods, fairies, heart transplants and how two very different girls face traumatic events in their lives. Part of the story is told by Alice and is modern-day; the other is told by Flo and is set in the weeks following the end of World War One.